ALONE AND AFRAID

Lisa collapsed flat on the ground on her stomach, squeezing her eyes shut tight as she waited for the shooting pains to subside again. What was she going to do? She was in a strange forest, far from any traveled trail, in the middle of a rainstorm. She couldn't walk, and even if she could, she wouldn't know which way to go. She buried her face in her uninjured arm and started to cry.

She was sobbing so loudly that she almost didn't hear the sound coming from directly above her. A soft, tentative sound, almost lost in the pounding of the rain and the whistling of the wind through the treetops. A familiar sound. Lisa stopped crying. Could it be?

Gathering all her strength, she rolled onto her side and looked up. A pair of large, soft brown eyes stared back at her. Then the sound came again: a whuffling nicker.

"Tiny!" Lisa cried to the horse. "You came back!"

THE SADDLE CLUB

HORSE CARE

BONNIE BRYANT

A SKYLARK BOOK
NEW YORK • TORONTO • LONDON • SYDNEY • AUCKLAND

RL 5, 009–012

HORSE CARE

A Bantam Skylark Book / April 1998

ISBN 0-553-48626-8

Published simultaneously in the United States and Canada.

PRINTED IN THE UNITED STATES OF AMERICA

OPM   0 9 8 7 6 5 4 3 2 1

*I would like to express my special thanks
to Catherine Hapka for her help
in the writing of this book.*

LISA ATWOOD GLANCED at her watch as she hurried up the driveway of Pine Hollow Stables. "Rats," she snapped, even though there was no one around to hear her. She broke into a jog.

When she reached the main stable building, she swung open one of the big double doors and went inside. Then she glanced at her watch again. She wasn't going to be late for her Pony Club meeting. That was a relief. She hated being late, even for appointments she set for herself. And today she had planned to spend some time with Prancer, the mare she usually rode, before her Pony Club meeting. Why had her mother chosen this morning—right before Horse Wise—to break her rotten news?

"At least it's not a mounted meeting," Lisa muttered under her breath as she rounded the corner into the U-shaped stable aisle.

Horse Wise, Pine Hollow's Pony Club, met every Saturday morning. The meetings alternated between mounted and unmounted sessions. At the mounted meetings, the students practiced their riding and learned new skills. At the unmounted meetings, they learned about all aspects of horse care, from grooming to veterinary care to stable management. Today's meeting was an unmounted one, which meant that Lisa didn't have to tack up Prancer, which meant that she still had a few free minutes before she had to head to the indoor ring.

When Lisa reached Prancer's stall, the tall, elegant-looking Thoroughbred was munching quietly on a mouthful of hay. When she saw Lisa, she pricked her ears forward and let out a snort.

"Hey there, girl," Lisa whispered, reaching over the half door of the stall to stroke the horse's glossy neck. Just seeing Prancer made her feel a little calmer. She let herself into the stall and went about giving the horse a quick grooming.

A few minutes later she reluctantly said good-bye to Prancer. "Sorry to groom and run," she told the horse with a final pat. "I'll make up for it after the meeting. I promise."

Lisa left the stall and went to find her two best friends.

She found them exactly where she expected to find them—in the stalls of their own horses.

Carole Hanson was spreading fresh straw on the floor of a large box stall while her horse, Starlight, waited patiently in cross-ties in the aisle. Stevie Lake was letting herself out of the stall next to Starlight's. Stevie's horse, a lively mare named Belle, was nibbling at her owner's sleeve as if to hold her back.

"Stop it, Belle," Stevie said, giggling, as she pushed the horse's head away and swung the half door closed. "I already told you, you big goofball. You can't come to the unmounted meeting. Not even if you sit in the back and keep quiet."

Despite being distracted by her own worries, Lisa couldn't help smiling at the image of Belle sitting on a bench in the indoor ring, listening to a lecture on horsemanship. "I don't know about that," she said. "Maybe if you put one of those fake-nose-and-glasses disguises on her, Max might think she was just a visiting student from another stable." Max Regnery was the owner and manager of Pine Hollow, as well as the girls' riding instructor. He definitely was *not* the type of person who would fail to notice if a horse showed up where it wasn't supposed to be, disguise or no disguise.

Stevie looked up. "Hi, Lisa. Hey, that's not a bad idea," she said with a grin. "Come to think of it, I have one of those disguises in my cubby."

3

Carole rolled her eyes. "Why doesn't that surprise me?" Stevie's sense of humor was legendary. She loved to play pranks and practical jokes of all kinds.

Carole and Lisa weren't nearly as mischievous as Stevie most of the time. But that hadn't stopped the three of them from becoming best friends and forming The Saddle Club. The group had only two rules: Members had to be horse-crazy, and they had to be willing to help each other out however and whenever help was needed. Sometimes the girls' different personalities meant they provided different kinds of help. Stevie was always ready to suggest impulsive solutions to problems. Lisa usually had sensible, well-thought-out ideas. And Carole, the horse-craziest of the three girls, almost always managed to involve horses somehow.

"Come on, let's get to the meeting," Carole said, glancing at her watch. "I want to get a good seat."

"Do you know what it's about?" Stevie asked, latching Belle's stall door.

"Max didn't say last week." Carole led Starlight back into his stall. Then she leaned out to add, "But a little bird told me Judy's coming to speak."

Judy Barker was a local vet who took care of the Pine Hollow horses. Carole sometimes volunteered after school as her assistant, accompanying her on her rounds of the area's stables and farms.

"Did she tell you the topic?" Stevie asked, reaching

into Belle's stall to tickle the mare playfully in her favorite spot.

Carole shrugged as she emerged from Starlight's stall and closed the door. "No," she said. "She says it's a surprise. But she promised it would be interesting."

"Maybe I should have asked Phil to come this week," Stevie mused. Horse Wise members were allowed to bring guests to unmounted meetings, and Stevie sometimes invited her boyfriend, Phil Marsten, who lived about ten miles away and rode at a different stable. "That reminds me," she said with a sudden frown. "I was all set to beg Max to make a special exception so that Phil could come to next week's mounted meeting. But before I could come up with a good story, Phil told me he can't make it." She shrugged, looking annoyed. "Something about his sister's birthday party."

"What a silly excuse," Carole said jokingly. But she could understand why Stevie was disappointed. Max had already announced that he would spend next week's Horse Wise meeting working with the more advanced older riders on the pirouette, a challenging dressage move, while the younger riders worked with Red O'Malley, Pine Hollow's head stable hand and a great rider and teacher in his own right. All three members of The Saddle Club were excited about improving their pirouettes, in which the horse must complete a full circle with its front hooves while keeping its back hooves in one spot. Stevie was the most excited of all. She was very interested in dressage and loved to practice it. "And how inconsiderate of his sister," Carole went on. "What nerve, being born on the same day as a Horse Wise meeting."

Stevie was still looking grumpy, but she couldn't help laughing. "Ha," she said. "Very funny."

Carole winked at Lisa, then turned back to Stevie. "Don't worry," she said. "Once Phil hears you're working on a pirouette at the walk, he'll find a way to work on it himself and do it at the canter. Just to make sure your relationship stays interesting."

Stevie grinned. She and Phil were both very competitive, a trait that had almost ruined their relationship more than once. But by now they had learned not to take things so seriously—most of the time, anyway. "Very funny," Stevie said again, sticking out her tongue at Carole. "You don't know what it's like. Just wait until you have a boyfriend. A very busy boyfriend who never has time for you."

Carole laughed. She could tell Stevie was joking. "Hey, no problem," she said. "As long as what he's busy with most of the time is horses, I'll be satisfied." She glanced over at Lisa for support, but Lisa was staring blankly at Starlight.

Stevie noticed, too. "Uh, Lisa?" she said. "Earth to Lisa! Come in, Lisa!"

Lisa blinked, then glanced at her friends. "Oh!" she

said. "Sorry about that. When you mentioned next week's meeting, I guess I kind of spaced out." She took a deep breath. "You see, I just found out I won't be able to make it."

"What!" Stevie exclaimed, knocking over Belle's grooming bucket. She hardly noticed when the brushes and rags and currycombs scattered across the floor. "What do you mean, you can't make it?" Such a thing was unheard of. Nothing short of a major vacation or serious illness kept a member of The Saddle Club away from Pine Hollow on a Saturday morning.

"I was pretty stunned myself when my mom told me," Lisa said grimly.

"Explain," Stevie said simply, picking up the grooming tools.

"My mom made a new friend at one of her volunteer committee meetings," Lisa said. "Her name is Mrs. Mills, and she lives over in Colesford." That was the name of a town about twenty miles from Willow Creek, Virginia, where The Saddle Club lived. "She invited my parents to some kind of fancy all-day charity auction and party next Saturday."

"What does that have to do with you?" Carole asked. "If your mom is worried about your being home alone, you can come and stay with me."

"Great idea," Stevie said. "Why don't we make it a sleepover? We can make popcorn, watch movies . . ."

"Talk about pirouettes," Carole supplied. "Maybe

call up Phil and taunt him about not being able to do one."

Stevie grinned and tossed a rub rag at Carole. "And figure out where to find Carole a boyfriend who's even horse-crazier than she is," she teased. "If that's possible. Which I doubt, unless you're talking about a member of the Olympic Equestrian—"

"Stop!" Lisa interrupted, a little upset. Her friends already seemed to have forgotten what they were supposed to be talking about. "That's not the problem. The problem is that I'm supposed to go to Colesford with them and spend the day hanging out with Mrs. Mills's daughter, Marguerite."

Carole looked confused. "Why?" she asked. "You don't know her, do you?"

"Of course not!" Lisa felt frustrated. Sometimes the three members of The Saddle Club seemed to know each other so well that they could read each other's minds. This clearly wasn't one of those times. "Don't you get it? My mom is so impressed with Mrs. Mills that she's sure Marguerite is just the right kind of friend for me to have. So she volunteered me to go riding at Marguerite's stable in Colesford and then hang out with her all evening until the adults get back from their fancy party—even though it means I'll miss Horse Wise *and* our jump lesson afterward."

Carole wasn't sure why Lisa looked so angry. It was definitely disappointing to have to miss a day at Pine

Hollow—especially a day when they would be learning something so interesting. But the alternative didn't sound as horrible as Lisa seemed to think it was. "At least Marguerite is a rider," she offered tentatively. "It might be fun to try a new stable."

Stevie nodded. "And you never know," she added. "Marguerite might be nice." She shrugged. "I'm sure Max will forgive you for missing one Horse Wise meeting. Maybe. If you muck out about a million stalls and promise to mix the grain for an entire year."

Lisa could tell that her friends were trying to cheer her up. Maybe they had a point. Maybe she was making too much of this because she was angry that her mother hadn't consulted her. She shouldn't take that anger out on Marguerite Mills—or on the rest of The Saddle Club, either.

Lisa did her best to smile. "Well, maybe you're right." She bent to retrieve a dandy brush that Stevie had missed and tossed it into the bucket. "My mom said she told Mrs. Mills about how I like to ride, and Mrs. Mills says Marguerite spends just as much time at her stable as I do here."

"Where does she ride?" Stevie asked.

"Fox Crest Farms," Lisa said. "I've never heard of it, have you?"

Carole shook her head. "I guess they're not on Judy's list of patients."

"Well, my mom seems to think it's *very* exclusive."

Lisa rolled her eyes. "It's very small and probably outrageously expensive."

"Really?" Stevie said, looking interested. "Hmmm. Maybe we can convince our favorite local snob to start riding there instead of here. What do you think?"

Both of her friends knew exactly whom Stevie meant—Veronica diAngelo. Veronica came from one of the wealthiest families in town, and she thought that made her better than everyone else. She was always bragging about her expensive horse, Danny, or showing off her overpriced, custom-made riding attire.

Stevie continued without waiting for a response. "That could be the perfect solution," she said. "I mean, sure, Colesford is a bit of a drive from here. But I'm sure Veron—Hey! Ow! What did you do that for?"

Carole had just elbowed Stevie in the ribs. She did it again. "Shhh," she hissed. Then she nodded toward the end of the stable aisle. Veronica herself had just come around the corner.

Veronica spotted them immediately and frowned. "What are you three still doing here?" she said in her usual unpleasant tone. "Shouldn't you be in the ring sucking up to Max by now?"

Carole and Lisa didn't bother to respond. They didn't care if Veronica thought they were teacher's pets. They knew it was only because she was so careless about her responsibilities around the stable. Max expected all his riders to help out with chores, but Veronica had a real talent for making herself scarce whenever there was work to be done.

Stevie couldn't let the snobby girl's comment pass, though. "Hey, Veronica," she said. "Didn't you just wear those boots yesterday? I thought you had a new pair for every day of the year."

Veronica rolled her eyes. "Is that supposed to be funny, Stevie?" she said with a sneer. "That's pretty weak, even for you. Anyway, you'd better be a little nicer, or I might not tell you the fantastic news I just heard."

If there was one thing Stevie was sure of, it was that Veronica couldn't keep her mouth shut when there was gossip to spread. Usually her gossip was boring stuff about who was having a party or about the latest new couples at school. Still, Stevie thought, it was just faintly possible that Veronica had actually managed to find out the secret topic of today's meeting.

"What is it, Veronica?" Carole asked. Stevie could tell that her friend was thinking the same thing she was.

Veronica smiled. "Oh, it's no big deal," she said in a casual tone. "It's just that I heard we're getting a new student today. A boy. And I hear he's *incredibly* cute."

Stevie snorted. "Stop the presses," she said dryly. She glanced at Carole and Lisa. "Come on, we'd better get over to the ring. I think Judy's talk will be more interesting." She turned around to give Belle a good-bye pat, purposely ignoring Veronica.

Veronica looked annoyed. "Fine," she said. "I should

have known you three were too immature to appreciate my news." She spun on her heel and stomped away, not even pausing to look in on Danny, who was in a stall nearby.

"Do you think we're really getting a new student?" Lisa wondered aloud as Veronica disappeared around the corner.

Carole shrugged. "Who knows? She hardly ever gets her facts straight." She grinned. "If there really is a new boy joining Horse Wise, he's probably six years old."

"Good point," Stevie said. "After all, most of those younger kids really *are* pretty cute."

"Veronica seemed pretty excited about the whole idea of a new boy, though," Carole mused as the three started walking down the aisle toward the indoor ring. "I wonder if that means she's lost interest in Simon already." Recently Veronica had dated a Pine Hollow rider named Simon Atherton. When Simon had first come to the stable, he had been an awkward, gangly, nerdy boy who could barely stay in the saddle. Then his family had moved away. When Simon had returned a few months later, his riding skills hadn't improved much. But the rest of him had. He had become a tall, broad-shouldered, good-looking boy who could barely stay in the saddle.

Lisa gave Carole a look of disbelief. "You mean you actually haven't noticed?" she said. "Veronica gave up on Simon weeks ago. I guess she decided his family isn't socially prominent enough."

12

"Either that, or Simon finally realized what Veronica's really like," Stevie said. She turned to Carole with a grin. "Hey, that gives me a great idea. We were just talking about getting you a boyfriend. And Simon is free. What do you think?"

"*You* were just talking about getting me a boyfriend," Carole corrected. "And I think I'll pass on Simon. He may be a lot cuter now than he used to be, but his personality hasn't changed much. He's still kind of annoying." She giggled. "Maybe I'll take that cute new six-year-old instead."

Suddenly Carole noticed that Lisa was looking distracted again. "Lisa?" she said. "Are you still with us?"

Lisa sighed. "Yes," she said. "I was just thinking, that's all."

"About how Carole will be going off to college while her boyfriend's still in middle school?" Stevie guessed.

Lisa didn't even notice the joke. "No," she said. "I was thinking about how my mom still doesn't understand how important Pine Hollow is. Not just riding, but riding *here*. She thinks that just because I'll be in the saddle next Saturday, I've got nothing to complain about."

Carole nodded sympathetically. She knew exactly how Lisa felt. She had ridden at lots of different stables, and Pine Hollow was special. "Did you explain that to her?"

"I tried," Lisa said, "but she just kept talking about

13

this charity auction. She's really excited about it. I guess it's a big deal to be invited. Socially, I mean." She sighed.

As the three girls reached the end of the stable aisle, a horse looked out of the extra-large box stall on the corner and let out a whinny.

Carole paused to pat the horse. "Hi there, Calypso," she said. "How are you feeling?"

"She's probably excited," Stevie guessed. "I bet she already has her baby's name all picked out."

Calypso, a young Thoroughbred mare, was due to foal in the next few weeks. Max had bought her to breed with his stallion, Geronimo. The Saddle Club had been following the course of Calypso's pregnancy for months.

"She seems a little bored," Carole said, looking worried. "Maybe we should spend some extra time with her after the meeting."

Lisa gave Calypso a pat, too. "Good idea," she said. "But right now we'd better get going. If we're late, the only thing we'll be spending time with afterward is a manure fork."

"Okay, I'll start with an easy one," Judy said at the Horse Wise meeting. The topic had turned out to be equine pregnancy and foaling. "Who knows how long the average mare's gestation period is?"

Carole's hand shot up immediately. She had seen a lot of pregnant mares and assisted at several births, so she knew quite a bit. For one thing, she knew that when Judy asked about a mare's gestation period, she was talking about the length of her pregnancy.

All around the room, a lot of other hands were also waving in the air. The question was a pretty basic one. Judy pointed to Polly Giacomin.

"Polly?" Judy said.

"Eleven months," Polly said. "Approximately."

"That's right," Judy said. "Gestation typically lasts a little more than eleven months. Anywhere from around 320 to 360 days can be considered normal." She turned and glanced toward the doorway of the indoor ring. "Just a second," she said. "It looks as though our special guest has arrived."

Carole turned to see Red O'Malley standing just inside the doorway. He was holding a lead line with Calypso at the other end.

"Bring her in, please, Red," Judy called.

The stable hand led Calypso slowly toward the spot where Judy was standing. The Saddle Club exchanged glances. Carole smiled as she shifted to a more comfortable position on the sawdust-covered floor of the indoor ring. She could tell that her friends were thinking the same thing she was—now they didn't have to worry about Calypso being bored!

A few Horse Wise members scooted aside to give Calypso room. She moved slowly, and Red let her choose her own pace. The mare seemed to place every hoof carefully as she walked.

"Wow," Simon Atherton commented loudly. "She looks even huger out here than she does in her stall, doesn't she?"

A few of the other students snorted or giggled. It was just the kind of ridiculous comment that Simon always made. Still, Carole had to admit that she knew what he meant this time. Calypso looked gigantic. Her belly was taut and swollen and looked ready to explode.

Carole studied the mare, observing the way she moved and trying to see whether her udder had begun to increase in size, which would be a sign that the foal was coming soon. But she couldn't see any such changes yet.

Before long Calypso was standing at the front of the group. Red kept a good grip on her halter, but the mare didn't seem interested in acting up. She stood quietly, her ears flicking back and forth.

"All right," Judy said. "I think you all know Calypso, our resident mother-to-be. And I hope you've all been following her progress during the past few months."

Carole nodded. She had made a point of looking in on the mare as often as she could. All around her, she could see others nodding, including Stevie and Lisa.

"Good," Judy said. "I've been following this pregnancy closely, too. And it looks like Calypso's gestation is going smoothly this time."

For a second, Carole just nodded again. Then she frowned. *This time? What did Judy mean by that?* Calypso was a young mare, and this would be her first foal. Carole exchanged glances with her friends. A few other students were murmuring as they, too, wondered about the comment.

"Oops." Judy shot Max a guilty glance. "I guess you all didn't know. Calypso had some trouble the first time

Max bred her. She lost the pregnancy early on. That's not uncommon—it happens with up to twenty percent of mares."

Carole gasped. She couldn't believe it. She couldn't believe that something that important had happened and she hadn't even known.

Stevie was just as shocked as Carole. The members of The Saddle Club spent practically all their free time at Pine Hollow. It was incredible that they hadn't known about this. Stevie raised her hand. "What happened to make her lose the foal the last time?"

Judy shrugged. "It's hard to say," she said. "It wasn't anything specific in Calypso's case as far as I could tell. Some common reasons include problems with the embryo, advanced age in the mare, or even just plain stress."

"Stress," Carole whispered to herself. She gazed at Calypso. The mare certainly didn't look stressed at the moment. Her eyes were half closed and she seemed to be falling asleep. Still, Calypso was a Thoroughbred, and like many Thoroughbreds she could be high-strung. Could stress have caused her problems last time? The stable was awfully busy and noisy a lot of the time, with riders rushing around and horses coming and going.

Judy was still talking. "As I said, that loss wasn't especially unusual. However, we know that Calypso's dam had some trouble during all of her pregnancies, so we're keeping a close eye on Calypso just in case she has similar problems."

Judy went on to discuss other aspects of mare care, but Carole wasn't really listening. She was still staring at Calypso, thinking hard. She could hardly believe that Max and Judy hadn't said anything before about Calypso's first pregnancy. Now that she knew, it seemed more urgent than ever to help look after the mare as her foaling time grew near. She decided to talk to her friends about it after the meeting. Maybe they could make Calypso a new Saddle Club project. They could spend time with the mare, soothing her and keeping her company. They could see that she got the proper amount of exercise—Carole knew that pregnant mares needed to stretch their legs regularly, just the same as other horses. Maybe she would even talk to Max about moving Calypso to a quieter stall. He had probably put her in the corner stall to make it easier to keep an eye on her. But if The Saddle Club promised to check on her frequently, he might agree to give her more privacy.

Once she had decided on her course of action, Carole tuned back into Judy's lecture. The vet was listing some of the ailments that could strike a pregnant mare, along with their symptoms. Carole already knew about most of the problems, but hearing them listed all together was a little disheartening. The list seemed to go on and on. Anatomical or genetic defects. Tumors. Infections.

Breech births. There was so much that could go wrong! It was a wonder any foals were born at all.

Finally, Judy gave Calypso one last pat and nodded to Red. "I think that's enough for today," she said. "I hope you've all learned something new. And I hope you'll all be waiting as eagerly as I am for the arrival of Calypso's foal."

Max stepped forward. "Thanks, Judy," he said. "You've been very informative, as always." He looked out at the students. "We've still got about thirty minutes left of this meeting. We'll continue in just a moment. Keep it to a dull roar, okay?"

He hurried over to help Red with Calypso. Stevie turned to her friends, looking somber. "Are you two thinking what I'm thinking?"

"Only if you're thinking we have a new Saddle Club project on our hands," Lisa said. "We have to do everything we can to help Calypso through the rest of her pregnancy."

Stevie nodded eagerly. "I was thinking about what Judy said about stress," she said. "I wonder if that corner stall is really the best place for Calypso. We should talk to Max about it."

Carole smiled at her friends. She should have known they would have the same ideas she had. "I was going to suggest the same thing," she said. "Max might let us move her to someplace quieter if we promise to keep a close eye on her. I mean, we've helped take care of pregnant mares before, right? We can definitely help guide Calypso through this."

Stevie and Lisa nodded. "Definitely," they said in one voice.

"OKAY, CAROLE, IT'S your turn," Max said a few minutes later. He glanced at his clipboard. "Here's your question. Name at least five kinds of plants that are poisonous to horses if ingested."

Stevie crossed her fingers on her friend's behalf. Carole was winning the new game Max had invented, but Stevie figured she could still use a little extra luck. As with all Max's games, this one tested students' knowledge of horse care. First he'd asked all the students to line up across the center of the ring. Then he'd started going down the line, asking each student a question from the list in his hand. A correct answer earned one step forward. An incorrect answer meant a step backward. If a student ended up more than three steps behind the starting line, he or she was disqualified.

So far it had been a challenging and exciting game. Simon and a couple of the younger riders had been knocked out within the first few rounds. Many others had spent most of their time hovering around the starting line, taking as many steps backward as forward. Even Lisa, who normally did well at this sort of game, had been disqualified after a few minutes. Stevie was pretty sure it was because Lisa was still distracted by her conversation with her mother. But she didn't have much time to think about it, because Max kept her busy answering question after question.

The questions grew harder as the game went on, and before long only half a dozen players were left. Carole was about halfway to the finish line Max had marked across the ring. Nobody else was even close to catching up to her. Stevie herself was just two steps ahead of the starting line.

Carole thought for a second about the question Max had just asked. "Well, let's see," she said. "There's rhododendrons and azaleas. They can both cause a bad case of colic. And yew trees are really poisonous."

Max nodded. "That's right," he said. "Three down, two to go."

"Um . . ." Carole paused.

Stevie crossed the fingers on her other hand. Belle was allergic to several kinds of weeds, so Stevie knew more than most people about horses' reactions to plants. Like any good rider, she could recognize the most common poisonous plants and trees by sight. But she wasn't sure she could come up with two more names off the top of her head. It was the kind of thing she usually looked up in a book if she needed to know it.

"I've got another one," Carole said. "Oleander shrubs."

Max nodded. "I need one more." He glanced at his watch. "Five seconds."

"Um . . . ," Carole said, "I know I know some more. There are a couple of trees that can be poisonous, like that one that turns red in the fall. . . ."

"I need a name," Max said with a smile. "Three seconds."

Stevie held her breath. Carole hadn't missed a single question yet. Would she have to take a step back? It didn't seem fair. Stevie would bet her entire allowance for a year that Carole could pick out any poisonous plant she passed along a trail. You didn't have to know their names to keep your horse from eating them. Why should she have to know them now?

At that moment a voice came from the doorway. "Do you mind if I jump in and help her out? I think I know a few more."

Stevie turned along with everyone else to see who had spoken. There was a boy about her age leaning against the wall by the doorway. He was dressed in riding clothes, and he was one of the cutest boys she had ever seen. He had sparkling brown eyes, a wide smile, and jet black hair.

Max didn't look as surprised as everyone else at the new arrival. "Hello, Tate," he said. "I'm glad you could make it today after all. Welcome to Horse Wise." He turned to address the group. "Everyone, this is Tate Ryan. His family just moved to town, and he'll be riding here at Pine Hollow."

Out of the corner of her eye, Stevie saw Veronica give

23

her a smug look, but she didn't acknowledge it. So Veronica had been right for a change. So a gorgeous new boy had turned up to join Horse Wise. Big deal.

Tate grinned and gave a little wave. "Hi there, everyone." He turned his grin toward Carole. "You seem to be having a little trouble. Mind if I jump in? The tree you're trying to think of is the red maple. In summer and fall, the leaves can cause jaundice and anemia in horses."

"That's it!" Carole said, looking appreciative. "I just couldn't remember the name. I get all those trees mixed up—you know, maple, beech, oak—"

"Actually, oak leaves are bad for horses, too," the new boy broke in. "So are the acorns. They can cause liver damage and other problems." He moved farther into the ring and kept smiling at Carole. "Also, you didn't mention mountain laurel—that can cause colic or diarrhea, which is why one of its common names is sheep kill. Then there's locoweed or sorghum or Russian knapweed."

Stevie's jaw dropped. Up ahead, she could see that Carole looked just as surprised as she felt. *Russian knapweed?* Stevie had never even heard of the stuff.

Tate wasn't finished. "And, of course, there's deadly nightshade, also known as belladonna. That's poisonous to horses, just like it is to people. Even buttercups are mildly poisonous to horses. But only when the plant is alive. Once it's dried it's not a problem."

Carole just kept staring at Tate, her mouth open, but Stevie was grinning. The boy had sounded exactly like Carole launching into one of her lectures! Had Carole just met her match?

Max was smiling and nodding at the new boy. "Those are all correct, Tate," he said. "I can see that you're going to be a fine addition to our group." He gestured toward the starting line. "We were just playing a little game. Would you like to join in?"

"Sure," Tate said, stepping forward eagerly.

Carole finally closed her mouth. She even managed to give Tate a friendly smile, though she still looked a little stunned. She turned to Max. "Shouldn't we start over?" she asked. "It's not fair to make Tate start at the beginning."

"Don't worry about me," Tate said before Max could answer. "I'll do my best to catch up. It's just a game, right?" He listened and nodded as Max quickly explained the rules. "Got it," Tate said. "Fire away."

TEN MINUTES LATER, the unthinkable had happened. Tate was within one step of catching up to Carole. Stevie couldn't believe it. She was now a step behind the starting line, thanks to a tough question about the equine skeletal system. Andrea Barry, one of the best riders in Horse Wise, was only a step ahead of her. Polly Giacomin, Adam Levine, and several other students who had been riding for a long time had all been disqualified. Max's questions were really hard.

But Tate hadn't missed a single one since joining the game. He seemed to know everything there was to know about horses and riding.

Max looked down at his list again to find another question for the new boy. "Okay, Tate," he said. "I want to know the proper name of a horse's tailbone."

Stevie groaned. It was a pretty obscure question, even for Max. She was glad that Carole hadn't gotten it.

Tate didn't seem fazed at all. He didn't even pause to think before answering. "The caudal vertebrae," he replied calmly.

Max seemed a little surprised. "Correct," he said. "All right, Carole. Here's yours. Name at least five tools that you would find in a farrier's kit."

Carole nodded, looking relieved. The question wasn't a particularly difficult one. The farrier, or blacksmith, was a familiar sight around the stable. So were the tools he used. "Okay, there's the rasp," she said. "And a hammer. And a hoof knife. And a buffer. And, um, what's that thing called? . . ."

Max waited to give her a chance to think of the answer. But after ten seconds had passed, he finally shook his head. "Sorry, Carole."

She took a step back, looking embarrassed. She didn't miss another question after that, but neither did Tate. A few minutes later, he stepped across the finish line—first.

Max smiled at the new boy. "Congratulations, Tate. It looks like you're our new champion."

"TATE IS AMAZING, isn't he?" Stevie commented.

The meeting had ended, and the three girls were sitting on their favorite hillside overlooking one of the paddocks. They were eating the sandwiches they had brought for lunch and watching Calypso, who was grazing in the paddock below.

Carole took a sip of soda and nodded. "He really knows a lot," she said. "I can't wait to see him ride."

"Well, that's true. But it's not exactly what I meant," Stevie said. "Or at least, not entirely."

Lisa had been lying back on her elbows, enjoying the feeling of the warm breeze blowing through her hair. It was early spring, and the weather had been very unpredictable lately, swinging from cold and rainy one day to warm and sunny the next. "What are you plotting now, Stevie?" she asked, detecting a familiar tone in her friend's voice.

Stevie shrugged and did her best to look innocent. "Me? Plot?" she said. "Never. I was just thinking about what Carole and I were discussing earlier today."

"What?" Carole asked. "You mean about Calypso?"

Stevie snorted. "You know, it's a good thing I'm here, Carole," she said. "Otherwise you really wouldn't think about anything except horses. No, I'm talking about you needing a boyfriend."

"Wait a minute," Carole protested. "I never said I *needed* a boyfriend. You did. And I *thought* you were joking."

"I was . . . then," Stevie said. "But that was before Tate showed up." She grinned. "Don't you get it?" She turned to Lisa and shrugged, as if what she was saying were so obvious that it hardly needed to be put into words. "Carole needs a boyfriend who's as horse-crazy as she is. And we just witnessed how horse-crazy Tate is. He's the one. I'm sure of it."

Before Carole or Lisa could respond, all three girls heard a loud voice.

"Right this way, Tate," Veronica called, hurrying into sight through the back door of the stable. "I'll show you the paddocks where we turn out some of the horses."

" 'We'?" Carole repeated in amazement. "Since when has Veronica ever turned out Danny herself? Usually she commands Red to take him out to the paddock for her."

"I'm surprised she even knows we have paddocks," Stevie said.

Veronica was too far away to hear them. But she *had* spotted them, and she didn't look happy about it.

"Oh," she said. "Never mind, Tate. It's kind of crowded out here. Maybe we should go look at the tack room instead."

"Don't be silly, Veronica," Stevie sang out. She dropped her sandwich and jumped to her feet, hurrying down the hill toward the newcomers. "There's plenty of room out here for all of us. And it's such a beautiful day. Who wants to be stuck in the tack room?"

Tate grinned at her. "My sentiments exactly," he said, allowing Stevie to drag him toward the others.

But Veronica wasn't giving up that easily. "No, really, Tate," she whined. She hurried after him. "Um, I need to go to the tack room for a few minutes. You see, I promised Max I'd—um—clean some bridles before our jump lesson this afternoon. And I'd hate to disappoint him."

Stevie started to laugh, but she managed to turn it into a cough. As far as she knew, the only time Veronica had been near the tack room all month was when Stevie had squirted her brand-new designer hunt vest with disappearing ink. That had sent Veronica running for the tack room sink. Stevie was pretty sure that Veronica hadn't stopped to clean any bridles while she was there.

"In that case, Veronica," Stevie said, trying to sound earnest, "we don't want to keep you. Why don't you go ahead and clean those bridles right now? We'll keep Tate company for you."

"What?" Veronica glared at Stevie. "Uh, I mean, that's okay. I'm sure the bridles can wait."

Carole smiled. "I don't know about that, Veronica," she said warningly. "You know how Max can be about stable chores. You don't want to make him mad, do you?"

Stevie almost laughed again. In one way, what Carole

29

had said was perfectly true. Max did expect all his riders to pitch in. It was the only way he could keep expenses down, and besides that, he believed that riders should learn about *all* aspects of horse care—even the ones that weren't much fun. Veronica couldn't care less about any of that, or even about making Max mad. But she obviously *did* care about impressing Tate.

"Oh," Veronica said helplessly. She shot Stevie one last dirty look, then turned to Tate with a flirtatious smile. "Well, maybe I should go take care of that," she said. "I want to do my part, after all. How about coming along and keeping me company, Tate?"

Tate had taken a seat on the sun-warmed grass beside Carole. He looked very comfortable. "Actually, Veronica," he said, squinting up at her, "if you don't mind, maybe I'll hang out here for a few minutes. It's such a nice day and everything."

Veronica scowled. "Fine," she snapped. "But if you ask me, it looks like it's going to rain any minute." She whirled and stomped away toward the stable building.

I'll eat my hard hat if she goes anywhere near the tack room, Stevie thought with satisfaction. She plopped down on the grass again and picked up her sandwich. A couple of ants had already climbed onto it, but she didn't care. She flicked them off and took a bite. She couldn't wait to start figuring out the best way to turn Carole and Tate into a couple.

She didn't need to bother. Tate and Carole were already smiling at each other. Lisa had returned to her previous activity—leaning back and gazing into the bright blue sky.

"You did really well in the game back there," Carole told the new boy admiringly.

"Thanks," Tate said, smiling wider and revealing a perfect set of teeth. Carole couldn't help noticing that he was even better-looking up close than he had been from a distance. "You did great, too, Carole. That question about the farrier's tools was pretty tough."

Carole nodded ruefully. "Not that tough, though," she said. "I remembered the word I was trying to think of as soon as the meeting was over. *Pritchel.*"

"I hate when that happens," Tate said cheerfully. "When I can't think of a word, I usually try to think of something else. The word I'm trying to think of comes to me eventually. For instance, instead of trying to come up with *pritchel*, you could have named some other farrier's tools, like pincers or hoof nippers or nail pullers."

Carole just nodded. She didn't want to admit it, but she wasn't sure she ever would have remembered all those tools, although she did now that Tate had listed them. She knew what they all were. She knew what they were used for. But she didn't have all the correct names on the tip of her tongue the way Tate obviously did. Was there no end to this boy's knowledge about horses?

She decided to find out. "So, Tate," she said, trying to sound casual, "before you got here, we were talking about Calypso." She gestured to the mare down in the paddock.

Lisa sat up and shot her a curious look. They hadn't been talking about Calypso before Tate arrived. They had been talking about Tate. She gave Stevie an amused glance.

Carole didn't notice. She was trying to remember some of what Judy had told them that day during Horse Wise. Since Tate hadn't arrived until after Judy had left, he wouldn't have heard any of it.

Carole decided to start with something fairly easy. "Um, we're helping Max take care of Calypso while she's pregnant," she went on.

Tate nodded, looking interested. "Really?" he said. "It's nice of you to do all that extra work."

"Oh, we don't mind," Carole assured him. "It's just that we were talking a minute ago, and we couldn't remember what Calypso should be eating at this stage of her pregnancy. Do you know if broodmares need a special diet?"

Stevie snorted. She knew that Carole didn't need any help with that question. For one thing, Judy had just gone over it in Horse Wise. But even if she hadn't, Carole had probably known all about the proper diet for broodmares before she was out of diapers herself.

Tate didn't seem to think the question was strange at all. He glanced down at Calypso. "Well, let's see," he said. "How far along is she?" When Carole told him, he nodded thoughtfully. "I see," he said. "So she's well past the first eight months. During that time, pregnant mares can get the same food as all the other horses. But now that she's into her last three months, she should be eating an increasing ration of grain. Also, you could give her a vitamin-mineral supplement."

Carole nodded. "That sounds good." She opened her mouth to ask a slightly more difficult question about show tack.

But Tate wasn't finished. "There's one very important thing to keep in mind, though." He held up one finger like a schoolteacher. "You shouldn't allow her to eat *too* much and get overweight. That can cause complications. And broodmares should be properly vaccinated to protect them and their foals—you know, equine influenza, strangles, tetanus, viral rhinopneumonitis. In this part of the country you'd probably need to vaccinate for Potomac horse fever as well, preferably about a month or so before you think she's most likely to foal, and . . ."

He went on, but Carole wasn't listening anymore. Neither were her friends. They were exchanging amazed glances. It sounded as if Tate were just warming up, as if he could go on about this topic for hours—maybe days. Just like Carole herself!

After he finally wound down, Carole asked Tate a few more questions. But she hardly needed to listen to his lengthy, precise, and enthusiastic replies. She already had the only answer she really wanted: This boy knew his stuff.

Finally, after discoursing for about ten minutes on the benefits of the straight bit versus the eggbutt snaffle in training young horses, Tate glanced at his watch. Then he stood up and brushed a few blades of new spring grass off his pants. "Well, I guess I'd better get going," he said. "It was really nice to meet you all. I'm sure I'll see you around real soon."

"Aren't you staying for the jump class?" Stevie asked.

Tate shook his head. "I wasn't sure I'd make it to the stable at all today," he said. "I should be at home helping my parents unpack right now. But Max is going to give me a few private lessons this week after school. I'm sure I'll be ready to join your riding class in no time at all."

Carole was sure of that, too. "That's great," she told Tate. "It's always fun to get a new student in class."

"Cool," Tate said. He gave The Saddle Club a wave and headed down the hill.

"See you soon," Stevie called after him cheerfully. "Real soon, we hope!" Then she turned and gave Carole a broad wink. "Definite boyfriend material," she said under her breath.

Carole ignored her, hoping that her words hadn't been loud enough for Tate to hear. Whether he had heard or not, she could still feel herself blushing. All this talk about boyfriends was ridiculous. Her friends knew how she felt about that topic. She wasn't ready to start seriously dating yet, let alone getting involved in a real one-on-one relationship.

Still, she couldn't help watching Tate as he strolled down the hill toward the stable. Maybe, just maybe, this was the boy who could change her mind about all that.

CAROLE BIT HER LIP and squinted as Stevie rode Belle in front of her. It was the following Wednesday afternoon. It had rained hard for most of the day while the girls had been in school, but now the sun had come out and was shining brightly over Pine Hollow's outdoor ring. Stevie and Carole were putting in some extra dressage practice with their horses. They wanted to be prepared for Saturday's Horse Wise meeting.

Carole gathered her reins and moved Starlight a step forward as Stevie brought Belle to a halt.

"Wait," she called to Stevie. "Try that half-pass again."

Stevie shrugged and started Belle trotting again. As Carole watched carefully, Stevie gave the signal for the half-pass, a common dressage move in which the horse moved diagonally forward and sideways.

"Well?" Stevie said after a moment. "How was that?"

"It was better that time," Carole said, trotting forward to join her friend.

Stevie frowned a little. "Better?" she said. "What do you mean? Did Belle mess up the first time? I didn't catch it."

Carole shook her head and smiled. "Belle didn't mess up," she said. "You did. You were leaning to the side."

"Really?" Stevie looked annoyed. But Carole could tell that Stevie's annoyance was with herself rather than with Carole. "That's funny. I haven't done that for ages. It's a beginner's mistake."

"Don't worry about it." Carole grinned. "Or as Max would say, don't worry about it, just fix it."

Stevie chuckled. "You're right. He *would* say that." She leaned forward to give Belle a pat on the withers. "He'd also say that it takes two to do dressage right—a well-trained horse *and* a well-trained rider. We're a team, right, girl? I shouldn't just let you do all the work to make us both look good."

"Speaking of teamwork, maybe we should take a break now and take care of our Saddle Club project," Carole suggested. She and Stevie had been working hard for almost an hour, and the horses were getting tired.

"You mean Calypso?" Stevie said. "Good idea. I

looked in on her when I got here and she seemed fine. But maybe we should take her out for a walk."

"That's exactly what I was thinking." Carole slid off Starlight's back and headed toward the gate. "Judy says it's good for pregnant mares to get regular exercise, even if it's just walking."

"In that case, maybe Lisa should have taken her to the mall," Stevie joked as she dismounted and followed Carole through the gate. "She's probably doing plenty of walking there. You know—from the clothing store to the shoe store, from the shoe store to the jewelry store, from the jewelry store to the department store, then back to the shoe store again—"

"Okay, okay," Carole interrupted. "I get the point." She giggled. "But somehow I don't think Calypso would fit in with Lisa and her mother. Mrs. Atwood would probably want her to get a makeover or something." Lisa's mother had dragged Lisa to the mall that afternoon to shop for new outfits to wear on Saturday. Once again, Lisa had tried to protest—she had been planning to practice dressage with her friends—but Mrs. Atwood wouldn't take no for an answer.

Stevie gave a mock shudder. "That would be horrible," she declared. "Can you just see poor Calypso with blue eye shadow and a curly perm?"

FIFTEEN MINUTES LATER, after putting their horses away and giving their tack a quick cleaning—what Carole's father

38

would have called a lick and a promise—Stevie and Carole met up again in front of Calypso's stall. Max hadn't wanted to move her, so she was still in the corner stall. But he had promised that if The Saddle Club saw any signs of stress, he would consider moving the mare someplace quieter.

The girls found someone else already at the stall. "Hello, Stephanie. Greetings, Carole," Simon said. He was leaning on the half door of Calypso's stall, watching the mare as she munched on a mouthful of hay. "Coming to observe the condition of the mommy-to-be?"

"Indubitably," Stevie confirmed. She wasn't sure what that meant, but somehow it seemed like the right response for Simon. Simon didn't talk like anybody else their own age. He was also one of the few people who called Stevie by her whole name. "What are you doing here?"

"The same thing you are," Simon said enthusiastically. He ran one hand through his wavy blond hair. "I can't wait until she has her foal. I've never seen a newborn horse before!" He lowered his voice and glanced around as if he wanted to be sure nobody could overhear. "And just between you and me, some of that stuff Judy was talking about the other day made me a bit nervous. I thought it might help if I kept an eye on Calypso until her baby's born."

Stevie bit the inside of her mouth to keep from laughing. Nobody in the state of Virginia knew less about horses than Simon, despite his earnest efforts to learn. He was hopeless. Still, Stevie reminded herself, his heart was in the right place. That was what counted. Besides, if things didn't work out with Tate, maybe Stevie could still convince Carole to go out with Simon. With Carole as a girlfriend, maybe Simon would actually turn into a decent rider. Anything was possible!

"We're keeping an eye on her, too," Stevie said, being careful not to catch Carole's eye. "You can help us if you want."

"Thanks, Stephanie," Simon said. "Gosh, that would be great. With all of us watching her, Calypso is certain to—"

"Hey there!" a cheerful voice interrupted. Tate had just rounded the corner. He was carrying an armful of riding clothes, topped off with the boots he'd been wearing the other day. Stevie noticed that he looked more handsome than ever in a pair of khaki pants and a rugby shirt.

"Hi, Tate," Stevie greeted him enthusiastically. She turned to give Carole a meaningful look. The girls had seen a lot of Tate since Saturday, but not enough for Stevie's taste. She had been disappointed when she discovered that Tate was in Lisa's class at school rather than Carole's. And she was even more disappointed when Tate hadn't shown up for the girls' riding lesson the day before. In fact, even though Tate had come to Pine Hollow almost every day, the girls still hadn't seen him ride. That part didn't really bother Stevie, though. Actually, she thought it was a good sign. It proved that Tate wasn't like Veronica—interested in riding but not in all the other things that went into horse care. He liked to be around the stable whether he was riding or not.

"Hi, Stevie," Tate said. "Hi, Carole. How's Calypso?"

"She's fine," Stevie said. "What have you got there?"

Tate glanced down at the things he was carrying. "I'm on my way to drop off some extra riding clothes and stuff. Max assigned me a cubbyhole." Each of the riders at Pine Hollow had his or her own cubby in the student locker room where he or she could keep spare clothes and shoes or stow schoolbooks while riding.

"Is that a hunting horn?" Carole asked in surprise, peering at a shiny copper item that was sticking out beneath a pair of breeches.

"It sure is." Tate pulled the item out to show her. It was a small copper horn with a nickel mouthpiece. "I got it for Christmas last year. Pretty cool, huh?"

Carole frowned slightly. The hunting horn *was* pretty cool. It was also a piece of foxhunting equipment that was completely unnecessary for anyone short of a professional huntsman.

Tate caught her expression and grinned. "I know, I know," he said. "You're wondering why on earth I have one of these. It's my parents. They're sure I'm going to ride off into the woods and get lost and that this horn

41

will be the only thing that will save me." He raised the horn to his lips and pretended to blow. "I'll sound the horn, and the cavalry will come galloping to the rescue."

Carole couldn't help laughing, though she was embarrassed that Tate had caught her frowning. "I don't know about that," she said. "We do have some deep woods around here, I guess, especially in the state parks. But we're really not *that* far out in the country. Most places, if you just keep riding long enough, you're bound to come out on an interstate highway or a shopping mall parking lot or someplace."

"I tried to tell my folks that, but they wouldn't listen," Tate said with a mock sigh. "They insisted I bring this horn and carry it every time I ride." He grinned and winked. "I think it will look great decorating my cubby, don't you?"

The girls laughed as Tate started to tuck the hunting horn back into the pile of clothes. But Simon was reaching out toward it.

"May I see that?" he asked eagerly. "Gosh, I never even saw a hunting horn before. I thought they looked more like trumpets."

Tate looked at Simon, seeming to notice him for the first time. "Um, sure, I guess you can see it," he said, handing over the horn.

Carole realized that they hadn't even introduced the two boys. In fact, she realized that as soon as Tate had arrived she had forgotten that Simon was there. "Tate, have you met Simon?" she said quickly.

"He's in Horse Wise, too," Stevie supplied helpfully. "He's been riding here at Pine Hollow for a while."

Tate looked the other boy up and down. "Oh," he said. "Hi."

"Hi, Tate." Simon handed back the hunting horn and gave the new boy a friendly smile. "You came to Horse Wise last weekend, didn't you? You did great in that game. You really know a lot about horses."

"Thanks," Tate said with a shrug. "I figure if you're going to learn something, you might as well really learn it. Otherwise, what's the point?"

Simon nodded. "I suppose," he said. "It's just so hard to remember everything sometimes. There's so much to know. I mean, I still have trouble remembering to keep my thumbs up and my heels down. Or is it my thumbs down and my heels up?"

Tate frowned and looked Simon up and down again. "How long did you say you've been riding?"

Carole was a little surprised at his tone of voice. He almost sounded disdainful. That wasn't fair. He should realize that different people learned at different rates. Just because Simon wasn't what you would call a natural-born rider, that didn't mean Tate should look down on him.

"So anyway," Stevie broke in, "I think we'd better pay some attention to Calypso now. She's probably lonely."

"Good idea, Stephanie," Simon said. "Should we check her over first? You know, look for some of those signs Judy told us about? Um, what were they again? Something about a waxy bag . . ."

"First you need to check whether the mare's udder is increasing in size," Tate said, frowning at Simon. "That's called bagging up. In her last week of gestation she may or may not get a little wax bead on the opening of her teats. That's called waxing up, and a lot of people think it happens in every mare's pregnancy. But it doesn't."

"Gosh," Simon said quietly. "I didn't know that."

"There's no reason you would," Carole said, putting a comforting hand on Simon's arm. "I don't think Judy mentioned it the other day in her talk." She gave Tate another surprised glance. He was looking self-satisfied. It was almost as though he had enjoyed proving how much more he knew than Simon. *Maybe he's not so perfect after all*, Carole thought uncertainly.

"I'd better go put this stuff away," Tate said. He gave Carole and Stevie a wide grin that showed off his even, white teeth. "Max is supposed to give me a lesson in a few minutes, and I heard he's a bear if you make him wait."

He sounded friendly again, and Carole wondered if she had been imagining things a moment before. Maybe Tate hadn't realized he was making Simon feel bad. He had probably just been trying to share his knowledge with someone who clearly needed it. Carole did that

44

herself all the time. In fact, sometimes her friends had to remind her that her extensive lectures weren't always welcome to every person in every situation. What if Tate was the same way? What if he was so eager to share what he knew that he sometimes forgot to be tactful?

Hmmm, she thought as Tate disappeared around the corner, *maybe we have more in common than I thought!*

AT THAT MOMENT Lisa was starting to wonder if she and her mother had anything in common. Mrs. Atwood had spent the last five minutes feeling the fabrics of two different wool sweaters, comparing the thickness and the drape. To Lisa, *drape* sounded like something that would be more important in curtains than in sweaters, but her mother seemed very concerned about it, so she kept quiet.

She sighed and leaned against a shelf of button-down shirts. It felt as though they had been in this department store for hours already. She didn't even want to think about how long they had been at the mall. Mrs. Atwood had insisted on buying Lisa three new pairs of white socks to wear under her low boots when she rode. Lisa had tried to explain that she already had plenty of white socks, and besides that, she would only be able to wear one pair on Saturday. Why did she need three? But her mother believed in being prepared—*over*prepared, as Lisa thought of it.

Finally Mrs. Atwood reached a decision about the

sweaters. "I really think this one is nicer, dear," she said. She picked a dark blue sweater from the pile on the shelf to her left. "And this shade will be just lovely with your coloring."

"I already told you, Mom," Lisa said with a sigh. "I have plenty of sweaters I can bring on Saturday. But I probably won't even need one. The weather has been so nice all week that I can probably just wear a long-sleeved T-shirt."

She felt a pang as she said it. After the rain had stopped that day, the weather had turned gorgeous—warm and bright and slightly breezy, perfect for practicing dressage at Pine Hollow.

Her mother shoved the blue sweater into Lisa's hands. "Don't be silly, dear," she said. "At this time of year, you never can tell what the weather will do. You don't want to get a chill while you and Marguerite are riding. Besides, this sweater will look much nicer than a T-shirt. You don't want Marguerite to think you don't know how to dress, do you? Now, let's go see if we can find a nice pair of trousers to go with that sweater."

"Trousers?" Lisa repeated. First her mother was ruining her weekend by making her go on this stupid visit. Then she seemed to want to humiliate her by turning her into an overdressed freak. She clenched her fists, trying to hold down her irritation. It wouldn't do any good to blow up at her mother, especially in public. Mrs. Atwood hated scenes. Instead, Lisa tried to make her voice sound as reasonable as possible. "Mom, nobody rides in trousers. Not even Marguerite Mills. I'll be fine in jeans."

"*Jeans?*" Mrs. Atwood looked horrified.

"Or jodhpurs," Lisa added quickly. She held up the blue sweater against her front and smiled appealingly. "Just think how nice this would look with that soft fawn-colored pair I have."

Mrs. Atwood thought about that for a second. Then she nodded. "Well, I suppose that would be all right," she said. "Do you think that's what Marguerite will be wearing, too?"

How should I know what Marguerite will be wearing? Lisa thought, though she just nodded and tried to smile at her mother as they headed toward the cash register. She was sick of hearing about Marguerite. Mrs. Atwood had been chattering about her all afternoon. Except when she had been talking about Fox Crest Farms. Or Marguerite's mother. Or the charity auction. Or the big party, which sounded like it was going to go on for half the night . . .

"Hey, Mom?" Lisa said. "I've been meaning to ask. What time will your party after the auction be over?" She crossed her fingers as she waited for the answer. Maybe if it was just a cocktail party like the ones her parents were always going to, it would be over by six o'clock or so. That might give Lisa time to meet Stevie and Carole for a quick Saddle Club meeting at TD's, an ice cream parlor in a shopping center near Pine Hollow. At least then she would get to hear about her friends' day—and blow off some steam about hers. She was sure she was going to need it if Marguerite was anywhere near as tiresome as Mrs. Atwood made her sound.

But Lisa's heart sank as she heard her mother's answer. "Oh, I'm not sure," Mrs. Atwood said cheerfully. "I imagine it will go until all hours. But I'm sure your father and I will be able to tear ourselves away in time to pick you up at Marguerite's house by ten o'clock or so."

"Ten o'clock at night?" Lisa said in dismay. "What am I supposed to do until then? Marguerite and I can't ride all day and all night."

Mrs. Atwood frowned. They had just reached the register, and she handed the sweater to the clerk. "Keep your voice down, Lisa," she said. "I don't understand what you mean. Surely you can spend time with an interesting young lady like Marguerite without being on a horse every second. I'm sure you two will find lots of things to talk about. And you really should appreciate that the Millses are opening their home to you so generously. You should be looking forward to spending the evening getting to know someone new."

Lisa sighed. In one sense, her mother was right—sort of. Normally Lisa wouldn't mind meeting someone new, especially another rider. It just didn't seem fair that she was being *forced* to do it. Not to mention being forced to miss an important Horse Wise meeting at the same time.

Besides, Marguerite sounded like a bore. What if she and Lisa didn't get along? As long as they were riding, they might be able to work around it. But what about afterward? According to Lisa's mother's plans, Lisa and Marguerite would be stuck together for hours and hours whether they liked it or not.

Lisa decided it was time to put her foot down. She waited until the salesclerk had taken her mother's credit card and moved aside to run it through the machine. "Listen, Mom," she said. "I have an idea."

"What is it, dear?" Mrs. Atwood asked. "Do you want to go look for a new pair of breeches for Saturday?"

"Jodhpurs," Lisa corrected automatically. "And no. My old ones will be fine. Actually, I was thinking that the bus runs pretty often between here and Colesford."

Mrs. Atwood looked suspicious. "I suppose that's true," she said. "But it doesn't matter. Your father will drive us there, of course."

"I know," Lisa said. "But I could catch a bus back to Willow Creek after Marguerite and I are finished riding. That way you wouldn't have to worry about leaving your party to pick me up. You can stay all night if you want to."

"Really, Lisa," Mrs. Atwood said. "I thought we'd settled this."

"No, listen, Mom," Lisa said. "It makes perfect sense. Marguerite and I can have a nice long ride at her stable. Then I can catch the bus back to town and walk home.

That will be a lot easier for everyone." *Especially me,* Lisa thought, but she didn't say it. "Especially for the Millses," she said instead. "We shouldn't impose on them too much, right? This way Marguerite won't have to worry about entertaining me all night." *And I can be back in time to meet my friends at TD's,* she thought hopefully. The local bus stopped at the shopping center, so she would be able to go straight there from Colesford. She held her breath and waited for her mother's response.

Mrs. Atwood paused for a long moment. She still looked disapproving. "Is that really what you want to do?" she asked at last.

Lisa nodded wordlessly.

Her mother sighed. "Well, I suppose if you've already made up your mind I won't try to change it. If you decide after your ride that you want to take the bus back, that will be fine. But your father and I will stop by the Millses' house on our way home just in case."

Lisa nodded. Her mother never gave up. "Thanks, Mom," she said. "Maybe Marguerite and I will hit it off. You never know what will happen."

"I'M SO JEALOUS," Lisa moaned. "I can't believe I'm going to miss it."

It was early Saturday morning and Lisa was sitting on the floor in the upstairs hall talking on the phone with Stevie. Stevie was getting ready to leave for Horse Wise. Lisa was getting ready to leave for her day with Marguerite Mills. She had brushed her teeth and her hair and put on the new blue sweater. Unfortunately, she had discovered a big manure stain on her jodhpurs that she hadn't noticed when she had worn them home from Pine Hollow the day before. There was no time to wash them before they left. Lisa hoped she would be able to convince her mother that everyone who was anyone at Fox Crest Farms probably wore jeans when they rode.

Otherwise, she had the funniest feeling they would be making a pit stop at the mall on their way to Colesford.

"You'll probably have fun, too," Stevie said. Lisa could tell she was trying to sound optimistic, but it wasn't very convincing. "Riding at a new stable is always interesting. And maybe Marguerite will turn out to be nice."

Lisa let out a snort. "Maybe," she said. "But I doubt it. She sounds like a total drip. And Fox Crest is probably totally snooty. My mom keeps talking about how exclusive it is."

"Hmmm." Stevie didn't seem to have an answer to that. "Well, anyway, at least your mom is letting you come home on the bus, right?"

Lisa nodded and twisted the phone cord around her finger. "Thank goodness," she said. "I'll definitely be at TD's by five-thirty, six at the latest. You and Carole will meet me there, right?"

"We'll be there," Stevie promised. "If all goes well, maybe we'll even have something interesting to report. You know, about Carole and her new boyfriend. I can tell she and Tate really like each other. But Tate isn't showing any signs of making a move, and Carole is still being wishy-washy about the whole thing. I've got a few new ideas to encourage them both—it'll be a lot easier once Tate is riding with Horse Wise. I hope he starts this week."

Lisa sighed. Stevie had been plotting all week to get

Carole and Tate together. Normally Lisa would have been interested in hearing about her latest schemes, but this morning all she could think about was the horrible day stretching ahead of her. "That's great, Stevie," she said morosely, picking at the carpet. "I wish I could be there to see it."

Stevie was silent for a second. "Listen, Lisa," she said at last, her voice more serious than usual. "I know you're upset about missing Horse Wise and everything, and I don't blame you. I'd feel the same way. But don't you think you should give Marguerite more of a chance? She might be nice, you know."

Lisa shrugged. Then she realized that Stevie couldn't see her, so she spoke. "I guess that's true," she said. "But I doubt it."

"She might be more than nice," Stevie went on. Now her voice sounded more the way it usually did—in other words, not serious at all. "She might be fantastic! She might be the coolest person you've ever met in your life. You might even decide you like her better than Carole or me, and that you want to start riding at Fox Crest, and transfer to the school in Colesford, and start some kind of Fox Crest Hoity-toity Club instead of The Saddle Club, and . . ."

By this time Lisa was laughing in spite of herself. Stevie could really get carried away. Then again, Lisa realized, so could she. She'd been so busy thinking about all the fun she would be missing that day at Pine Hollow that she hadn't really considered the possibility that she could have fun riding with Marguerite. *Or, at the very least, not be miserable,* she amended silently.

Aloud she said, "Okay, Stevie, I get the point. I'll wait until I meet Marguerite before I decide whether I like her or not."

"That's all I ask," Stevie said virtuously. "So anyway, getting back to Carole and Tate . . ."

At that moment Mrs. Atwood swept out of her bedroom wearing the fancy new linen suit she had bought at the mall. She was in the middle of fastening an earring in one ear, but when she saw Lisa sitting on the floor she stopped short.

"Aren't you ready to go yet?" she demanded. "And why are you wearing those jeans?"

Lisa held back a groan. "Stevie, I've got to go," she said. "I'll see you this afternoon, okay?"

"We'll be there," Stevie said. "Good luck."

"Thanks." Lisa hung up the phone and stood up. The battle of the blue jeans was about to begin.

"I'M STILL NOT sure about those jeans," Mrs. Atwood murmured, turning around to look at Lisa's legs from the front seat.

Lisa sighed. Her mother had given in on the jeans issue when she had seen the manure stain on Lisa's jodhpurs. But she wasn't happy about it. She had been making comments about Lisa's outfit all during the drive from Willow Creek.

Luckily Lisa's father spoke up this time. "Stop worrying so much, Eleanor," he said, sounding irritated. "I'm sure all the kids at that stable will be in jeans, too. That's all anyone Lisa's age wears these days. Even in high society."

Mrs. Atwood seemed ready to argue about that, but at that moment they passed a road sign reading WELCOME TO COLESFORD. "Oh, good," she said. "We're almost there. I don't want to be late."

Lisa leaned back against the car seat and sighed again. She glanced out the window at the sky, which was gray and cloudy. It matched her mood quite well, she decided.

A few minutes later her father was turning down a road that Mrs. Atwood had pointed out. Before long the car was pulling into a long, gently curving driveway leading to a large, whitewashed brick house.

"What a stunning home," Mrs. Atwood murmured.

Lisa didn't see anything stunning about it. It didn't look much different from the houses in their own neighborhood. Just bigger. But she didn't say anything.

As they stood on the front porch ringing the doorbell, Mrs. Atwood tugged at the back of Lisa's sweater, straightening the hem. "I wish you had taken my advice and braided your hair, dear," she whispered. "It would look much neater and more stylish that way, don't you think?"

The door opened before Lisa could answer. A girl about Lisa's age was standing there. "Hello," she said. "You must be the Atwoods."

"And you must be Marguerite," Mrs. Atwood said. She introduced herself, her husband, and Lisa. The whole time, Lisa could see her eyes traveling from the top of the girl's French-braided hair to the toes of her polished high boots, taking in a stylish wool sweater and a pair of spotlessly clean buff breeches along the way.

"Nice to meet you," the girl said. "Won't you come in? My mother is expecting you."

Lisa gave the other girl a weak smile as she trooped inside the house with the rest of her family. She was still trying to be optimistic. She really was. But it was getting harder every second.

". . . So I TOLD HER, I'm sorry, but I just don't give money to causes like that," Mrs. Mills said. "I donate to several respected charities on a regular basis, and I do quite a bit of volunteer work, if I do say so myself. I can't be expected to support every cause."

"Of course not," Mrs. Atwood said emphatically. "You do so much for the community as it is."

Lisa couldn't help grimacing. She leaned over her sherbet dish to hide her expression. The "cause" Mrs. Mills was talking about was an elementary-school girl selling candy bars door-to-door to raise money for new soccer uniforms. Lisa didn't think it would have hurt the woman to have bought a few. And whether she had or not, the topic certainly didn't seem to warrant a ten-minute discussion.

"Oh, let it go, Mother," Marguerite said, dipping her spoon into her sherbet. "You're just mad because that little brat's mother turned out to be on the school board and she told everyone you wouldn't contribute."

Mrs. Mills shot her daughter a venomous look. "Mind your manners, Marguerite," she said icily.

Mrs. Atwood leaned toward Lisa. "That goes for you, too, young lady," she whispered. "Stop hunching over your food like that."

Lisa sat up straight and glared at her mother. Would this lunch never end? Trying not to think about all the fun her friends were probably having back at Pine Hollow right then, she stirred her sherbet idly with her spoon and glanced at Marguerite out of the corner of her eye. Mrs. Mills had done most of the talking so far, so Lisa still wasn't really sure what the other girl was like.

Just then Marguerite turned toward Lisa. "So I'll bet you can't wait to see Fox Crest, right?" she said with a smile.

Lisa smiled back tentatively. "Sure," she said. This seemed promising. Maybe Marguerite was okay after all.

Mrs. Mills was nodding. "Oh, yes," she said compla-cently. "You'll love Fox Crest, Lisa. It's really a high-quality establishment. Marguerite tells me they have some beautiful horses, and, of course they cater to a very exclusive clientele."

Lisa glanced at Marguerite, expecting to see her roll her eyes, just as she would have done if her own mother had made a similarly shallow comment. But Marguerite was nodding in agreement.

"Definitely," she said. "I tried riding at another stable for a while, but it was awful. They let anybody who walked in off the street ride there, even if they showed up in ratty old jeans."

Lisa blushed and tried not to look down at her own jeans. They weren't exactly ratty and old. Compared to Stevie's jeans, which Stevie tended to wear until they fell apart, Lisa's looked practically brand-new. But Lisa had a feeling that the distinction would be lost on Marguerite.

Mrs. Mills cleared her throat meaningfully, and Marguerite suddenly glanced over at Lisa. She blushed, too. "Oops!" she said. "Oh, I'm sorry, Lisa. I didn't mean anything by that. Really. Um, actually, I was just admiring your jeans a moment ago. Where did you buy them? I might get a pair myself."

"I got them at the mall in Willow Creek," Lisa said. "I don't remember which store."

Mrs. Atwood broke in. Her face was brighter red than either Lisa's or Marguerite's. "I remember, dear," she said, obviously trying to sound cheerful. "It was that little boutique, wasn't it? Nouveau Style."

"Um, maybe," Lisa said. She knew very well that her jeans hadn't come from the expensive store her mother had mentioned. But she also knew that her mother was trying to save face in front of the Millses.

"Well!" Mrs. Mills said, in a too-bright, too-loud tone that meant she was trying to change the subject. "It looks as though everyone is finished. Shall we move into the sitting room?"

IT SEEMED LIKE hours later that the adults dropped off Lisa and Marguerite at the stable. Actually, Lisa thought, they had probably sat in the Millses' sitting room for only about twenty minutes.

By now, Lisa was sure that she and Marguerite Mills had very little in common. She had never met anyone as silly, shallow, and snobby as Marguerite—unless it was Marguerite's mother.

Even Veronica diAngelo can't hold a candle to those two, Lisa thought as she climbed out of the Millses' luxury sedan. Then she felt guilty. Marguerite might not be Lisa's idea of a good time, but at least she didn't seem mean and scheming like Veronica. *Probably because she's not smart enough,* a little voice in Lisa's head piped up before she could stop it.

Lisa pushed all such uncharitable thoughts out of her

mind as she followed Marguerite up a long landscaped drive toward a low, elegantly designed building.

"This is it," Marguerite said, sounding pleased. "Fox Crest Farms." She indicated the building with a sweep of her hand.

Lisa paused to take in the view. Just beyond the stable building she saw a gently rolling pasture where several sleek, healthy-looking horses were grazing. There was a mounting block near the front entrance to the building, and a man in formal riding attire was mounting a tall, strapping bay horse. Even with the sun still hiding behind the clouds, Lisa had to admit that it made a very pretty picture.

"It looks great," she said sincerely.

Marguerite smiled. "I know," she said. "Just wait until you meet the people. My friend Shannon will probably be here later—she has a full-blooded Arabian. And my friend Jack might be here, too. His parents own half the shopping malls on the East Coast. He rides a Thoroughbred."

Lisa couldn't resist speaking up. "I ride a Thoroughbred back at Pine Hollow," she said. "Her name is Prancer. She's really sweet and eager to please, and she—"

"Did I mention my friend Kelton?" Marguerite interrupted. She didn't even seem to realize that Lisa had spoken. "His dad's a senator, and Kelton has two horses: a Hanoverian and a Morgan."

Lisa didn't see why one boy needed two horses. After all, he could only ride one at a time. But she didn't say so. In fact, she gave up entirely on talking and just followed along quietly as Marguerite continued to reel off a list of her friends and their purebred horses.

Her monologue got a little easier to take once they entered the stable building and Lisa could see the horses herself. She didn't think she had ever seen so many beautiful horses in one place. Every single one seemed to be a purebred of one kind or another. More importantly, every one appeared well cared for and healthy.

As Marguerite led her on a quick tour, Lisa saw that the stable itself was a little smaller than Pine Hollow, but it was just as spotlessly clean. And Lisa knew that her mother would consider it a lot more elegant. Every stall had a large, polished brass nameplate by the door. The tack room had cedar-lined walls and fancy saddle racks. The people they passed were all dressed to the nines—even the ones Marguerite pointed out as stable boys.

After a while Lisa realized that she still hadn't asked Marguerite about her own horse. She quickly did so.

Marguerite smiled. "We're just getting to her stall." She hurried down the aisle they were in and paused beside a stall door. "Here she is. This is my horse, Amber."

Lisa looked into the stall and gasped. The horse inside was gorgeous. Amber was a light bay mare, about sixteen hands tall, with a refined head and lively, soulful eyes. She turned and gave Lisa a curious, intelligent glance, then returned to her previous occupation of picking at the hay in her hayrack.

"Do you like her?" Marguerite said complacently. "She's a purebred Trakehner. Those come from Germany, you know. In Europe."

Lisa knew that the Trakehner was a breed from Germany. As a matter of fact, she also knew that Germany was in Europe. But she kept quiet. She was busy looking at the horse. Amber was amazing.

For the first time, Lisa started to feel a little more positive about the day. She was starting to think that spending an afternoon riding one of these impeccably bred creatures could be pleasant.

"She's wonderful," she told Marguerite sincerely, reaching out to pat Amber's soft nose. "So, are you ready to ride?"

"Sure," Marguerite said. She headed toward the tack room.

Lisa followed silently for a few steps. She couldn't wait to find out which horse would be hers. Finally she cleared her throat. "Um, so who will I be riding today?"

Marguerite stopped short and gasped. Her hand flew to her mouth. "Oh, no!" she cried. "I knew there was something I forgot."

"What do you mean?" Lisa asked, confused.

Marguerite spun around and hurried down the hallway in the other direction, toward the offices she had pointed out earlier. "I'm so sorry, Lisa. I forgot to arrange a horse for you." She tossed Lisa an abashed grin over one shoulder. "But don't worry. I'm sure we can scrounge up something."

LISA SIGHED AND glanced up as she prepared to mount. "Okay, Tiny," she said. "Here we go."

The mare didn't respond to her name. Lisa didn't blame her. It wasn't exactly appropriate. Tiny was a large, heavy gray horse, swaybacked and slow-moving.

"Um, I didn't notice Tiny on the tour you gave me," Lisa said, trying to be tactful. She mounted, feeling her leg muscles stretch a bit. Tiny was a lot broader across the back than slender, athletic Prancer.

Marguerite shrugged. "I know," she said. "Her stall's way in the back. They don't like to keep her where people will see her. She's not exactly up to par with the other horses here, you know."

Lisa nodded, but she gave Tiny a quick pat, too. Tiny looked around and snorted as if in appreciation.

Lisa knew better than to write off a horse because of its appearance. Just because Tiny wasn't a gorgeous pure-bred like the other Fox Crest horses—and clearly not challenging enough for a good rider like Lisa—that didn't mean she was useless. "She must be handy for new riders," she commented.

"You're kidding, right?" Marguerite laughed. "Nobody

here would be caught dead on a horse like that. The only reason Tiny's here is because someone donated her as a tax write-off. She's so slow and dull that they take her along to shows and stuff to keep the other horses calm." She glanced over at Lisa as she swung aboard Amber, who was prancing and snorting and seemed full of energy. "I'm really sorry you're stuck riding her, Lisa. My mom is going to kill me when she finds out. But Mr. Keit said there just wasn't any other horse available right now."

"It's okay." Lisa settled her feet firmly in the stirrups and gathered her reins, preparing to start. Tiny was standing still, her head drooping. Every once in a while she let out a snort or a whinny, responding to things around her. Lisa smiled as the big horse nickered at a passing bird. "At least she's chatty."

Marguerite rolled her eyes. "Come on," she said. "Let's go." She sent Amber into a fast walk.

"Lead the way!" Lisa said, trying to sound cheerful. She signaled for Tiny to walk, and for a second the mare seemed reluctant to move.

Lisa was more than a little annoyed, though it had nothing to do with Tiny's laziness. She knew that none of this was the sweet old mare's fault. If Marguerite had done what she was supposed to, Lisa could have been riding a horse much more suited to her ability.

A strange, nagging feeling came over her as she followed the other girl out of the stable yard. She urged

Tiny into a ponderous trot to keep up with Amber's brisk walk. Something was bothering Lisa, but she couldn't figure out what was wrong. Then she realized what it was. She missed the lucky horseshoe.

The lucky horseshoe was a Pine Hollow tradition. It was nailed to the wall by the stable door, and Lisa, like all the riders at Pine Hollow, was always careful to touch it before setting out. No rider who had done so had ever been seriously hurt.

"Oh, well," Lisa whispered to Tiny, keeping her voice low so that Marguerite wouldn't overhear. "I should know better than to expect any good luck around here."

Tiny nickered and glanced back toward the stable building. Lisa smiled and gave her another pat. She could tell that the old mare didn't want to be out there any more than she did. Then Lisa glanced up at the sky. *Maybe Tiny and I will get lucky after all*, she thought hopefully as she saw still more gray clouds gathering at the horizon. *It looks like it's going to pour pretty soon. Then Tiny can get back to her hayrack, and I can get back to Pine Hollow early!*

"I'M STARTING TO wonder if Tate is ever going to ride with our class," Stevie grumbled. She and Carole were at Calypso's stall. The Horse Wise meeting and the girls' jump lesson had both come and gone, and there had been no sign of the new boy. The girls were on their way to the grain shed to mix the feed for the next week, but they had stopped by to see the pregnant mare first.

Carole could tell that Stevie was disappointed because Tate hadn't shown up. She had to admit, she was a little disappointed, too. But she was also relieved. Whenever the new boy was around, she felt kind of awkward. She wasn't sure whether that had anything to do with Tate himself or whether it was purely a result of Stevie's matchmaking. She decided it was time to change the subject. "The Horse Wise meeting was fun, wasn't it? Belle seemed to catch on quickly to what you were asking her to do."

Stevie's eyes lit up. "She did do well, didn't she?" she said. "Even Max said—"

Carole never got to hear what Max had said. Stevie was staring past her down the aisle, grinning widely. "What is it, Stevie?" Carole asked, turning to look.

"Hi there!" Tate called, walking toward them. "How's it going?"

"Tate!" Stevie exclaimed. "We're so glad you're here. We need your help. Max asked us to mix grain this week, and usually Lisa helps us, but she's not here today. We could really use an extra set of hands. How about it?"

Tate looked a little surprised, but he shrugged agreeably. "Boy, Max really is a slave driver, isn't he?" he said with a laugh. "Sure, I'll help you out."

Carole gave Calypso one last pat, then followed as the others headed down the aisle toward the feed shed. After a moment, Stevie dropped back and gave her a conspiratorial wink.

"What do you think?" she whispered. "This will give you some quality time to get to know each other. Especially if I have to step out for a while to go to the bathroom . . ."

"Don't!" Carole whispered back, her eyes widening.

Stevie just grinned, winked again, and hurried forward after Tate.

". . . AND THEN THERE'S wood shavings," Tate said happily, leaning back against a large sack of alfalfa pellets. "They're easy to find, and mucking out isn't a problem as long as you have a scoop and a shavings fork. They're comfortable, too, and most horses won't try to eat them. However, it's best to avoid oak shavings. There's tannic acid in oak, and that can be damaging to a horse's hooves. Then there's sawdust. . . ."

Carole sighed and scooped out another batch of bran to add to the mix she and Stevie were working on. Tate had been going on and on about stalls and bedding for what seemed like forever. Carole hadn't thought she could ever get tired of hearing about horses, but now she was beginning to wonder.

She was also beginning to wonder about Tate. Didn't he notice that neither she nor Stevie had spoken for at least ten minutes? Didn't he care? Or did he care more about showing off what he knew than talking to them? It also hadn't escaped Carole's notice that Tate wasn't helping much with the grains. Still, that might have been partly Stevie's fault. She had insisted on making Tate sit on a stack of empty burlap bags next to Carole, where he couldn't reach any of the ingredients except the barley. Since Max's feed mix didn't use much barley, Tate didn't have much to do.

"What's going on in here?" an unpleasant voice demanded.

Carole was startled out of her thoughts. She looked up and saw Veronica standing in the doorway of the grain shed, her hands on her hips and a suspicious expression on her face.

Tate grinned at her. "Hey, Veronica," he said. "How's it going?"

Veronica's expression quickly changed to a big smile. "Hello, Tate," she cooed. "I didn't know you were in here."

Yeah, right, Carole thought with disgust. She was sure that Veronica had known exactly where Tate was. Otherwise, why would she have bothered to come out to the grain shed?

Stevie seemed to be thinking the same thing. "Thanks for offering to help us, Veronica," she said sarcastically. "Luckily we've got everything under control. Oh, and I heard Max calling you a few minutes ago. You'd better go see what he wants."

Veronica shot her a poisonous glance. "That's okay, Stevie," she said smoothly. "I just talked to him. He asked me to supervise what you're doing in here."

Stevie glowered at her, and Carole bit back a laugh. She knew as well as Stevie did that there was no way Max would have asked any such thing.

Tate didn't seem suspicious at all. "Cool," he said, scooting over to make room for Veronica next to him.

"We were just talking about stable management and stuff."

"Oh, really?" Veronica sat down and then moved a couple of inches closer to Tate. She smiled at him and batted her eyelashes. "It figures. These two never want to talk about anything but horses, horses, horses. But I'd much rather hear more about you."

"Oh, really?" Tate smiled back at her. Without seeming to realize what he was doing, he reached into the barley bag and dumped a whole scoopful into the batch of feed they were working on.

Carole opened her mouth to protest, since that batch already had its full share of barley. But before she could, Stevie leaped to her feet.

"Hey!" Stevie shouted. "Did you hear that? I think it's your mom's car horn, Veronica. You'd better go check it out."

Veronica scowled. "You're hearing things, Stevie," she said. "I didn't hear a horn. Besides, I'm not getting picked up until later."

"I didn't hear anything, either," Tate put in. He dumped another scoopful of barley into the mix. "So anyway, Veronica, I heard you guys were working on the pirouette in your Pony Club meeting today. That's a fourth-level dressage move, you know. Some of the other moves added at the fourth level are . . ."

As Tate continued to talk, Carole was really getting annoyed. It was obvious that Tate wasn't paying attention to what he was doing. He was totally messing up the grain mix. He should know better. So should Stevie, for that matter. But she had dropped her scoop and was staring at Veronica with a determined look on her face.

"No, really," Stevie said loudly, interrupting Tate's monologue on the stages of dressage competition. "I'm sure I heard something. You'd better go check." She took a step toward the door to illustrate her point. Her foot hit the edge of an open bag of flaked corn, tipping it.

Carole leaped forward to catch it, but her own foot caught the edge of the metal bin they were using to mix the feed and sent her sprawling. The bin teetered for a second, then crashed to the floor, spilling its contents everywhere. Meanwhile, the bag of corn had fallen, too—landing right on Carole and covering her with dry yellow flakes.

"Oops," Stevie said with a weak grin.

Veronica stood up and gave the other two girls a disgusted look. "Nice going," she said snottily. "Look at the mess you've made."

Carole gritted her teeth and sat up, brushing corn flakes out of her hair. Stevie was staring at Veronica, speechless with fury.

Veronica didn't notice. She was reaching down to help Tate to his feet and smiling at him sweetly. "Come on, Tate," she said. "We'd better get out of their way so they can clean up after themselves."

71

Tate looked uncertain, but he shrugged and followed Veronica to the door. "Let me know if you need any more help later," he told Carole and Stevie as he left the shed.

"WHOA!" MARGUERITE CALLED with a laugh, pulling up on the reins. "Amber's really feeling her oats today!"

Lisa smiled weakly as she urged Tiny into a lumbering trot, trying to catch up to the other pair. They were riding down a wide, pleasant trail in the woods behind Fox Crest Farms. Amber was prancing along in the lead, clearly tired of walking and trotting. Tiny was doing her best to keep up. Lisa was appreciating the big mare's personality more and more with every step she took. Tiny was a little slow, but she wasn't as lazy as Lisa had first thought. She was eager to please, and her constant snorting, snuffling, and whinnying were kind of cute. It sounded as if she were talking to herself.

Still, when Lisa glanced forward at Marguerite, she couldn't help feeling a little envious. Amber was so beautiful and spirited. Why couldn't Marguerite have gotten her a talented horse like that? It would have made this whole afternoon—including Marguerite's self-centered prattle—a lot easier to take.

Lisa glanced up at the sky. The clouds were still there, and they seemed to be darkening. She opened her mouth to say something about the weather, but Marguerite spoke first.

"I've got an idea," she said brightly. "The trail looks pretty flat up there. Let's gallop!"

"What?" For a second Lisa was sure that Marguerite had to be joking. The trail *was* flat up ahead of them. But it was also winding, lined with stray branches, and littered with small rocks and twigs. It was perfectly fine for walking or trotting, but going at a faster gait would be asking for trouble. "I don't think so. It wouldn't be safe."

Marguerite twisted around in her saddle and gave Lisa a disgruntled look. "What do you mean?" she said. "It'll be fine. My friends and I gallop all the time. Come on, let's have some fun."

Lisa shook her head firmly. "It's not safe," she said. "The horses could break a leg."

"Oh, please." Marguerite rolled her eyes and rode on for a moment in silence. "Okay," she said suddenly. She twisted around again to look at Lisa. "If you won't gallop, let's have a walking race. Side by side. The first one to break stride loses."

Lisa hesitated. But then she shook her head again. "I'm sorry," she said. "But I don't think the trail is wide enough to ride side by side. There are a lot of branches hanging down—"

"Fine," Marguerite interrupted with a frustrated sigh. "We'll just ride along single file at a plain old trot. What a thrill." She urged Amber forward and was soon trotting far ahead.

Lisa sighed. Marguerite had been goofing off ever since they had started their ride half an hour before. First she had wanted to jump a pasture fence instead of going through the gate. Next she had wanted to ford a small but rapidly rushing river, while Lisa had insisted on crossing at the bridge she had spotted a little farther downstream. Lisa was starting to feel like Marguerite's parent, or maybe a strict riding instructor. But she wasn't about to let the horses—or herself—get hurt because Marguerite was too flighty to enjoy the simple pleasures of a trail ride.

"Hang in there, Tiny," Lisa whispered, giving her horse a pat. "She'll probably get bored soon and want to go back and hang out with all those exciting friends she keeps talking about. Then you can have a nice snack and a rest, and I can go home."

Tiny nickered and continued trotting heavily after the fleet-footed Amber. Lisa patted the horse again, then glanced at the sky. She urged Tiny forward, calling to Marguerite.

"What is it?" Marguerite asked, pulling Amber to a halt. Her irritation seemed to have passed, and she smiled at Lisa. "Hey, I have an idea—"

"Hold it," Lisa interrupted. She pointed at the sky. "Have you noticed those clouds? They're getting worse by the minute. Maybe we should turn back before we get caught in the rain."

Marguerite glanced up and then shrugged. "They

don't look that bad yet," she said. "Besides, we're only a ten-minute ride from the stable."

Lisa bit her lip. She wasn't really worried about the rain—Marguerite was right, the clouds didn't look too bad yet—but she really wanted to end this ride as soon as possible. If she was lucky, maybe she would be able to meet Carole and Stevie at Pine Hollow before they left for TD's.

Marguerite trotted off down the path. "Come on," she called to Lisa. "You know how crazy the weather's been lately. It probably won't rain at all."

"Probably," Lisa muttered, too quietly for Marguerite to hear her. "That would be just my luck."

The only answer was a sympathetic snort from Tiny.

TEN MINUTES LATER, Lisa was about to suggest turning back again when Marguerite brought Amber to a stop. "Check it out," the girl said.

Lisa followed her gaze. A narrow, overgrown trail led off at a right angle from the one they'd been following. "What is that?" she asked. "It looks like a deer track or something."

"It's one of the old trails," Marguerite said. "My friends and I saw it last time, but we didn't have time to follow it. We think it leads into the state park."

"Oh." Lisa glanced at her watch. "We probably should start heading back soon, don't you think?"

Marguerite didn't seem to hear her. She was staring

eagerly at the tiny trail. "Let's check it out," she said. "It looks like it gets a little wider up a ways, see? It'll be a hoot to follow it and see where it goes."

Lisa hesitated. She didn't think following the abandoned trail sounded like a "hoot" at all. It sounded like a sure way to end up with a lot of annoying little scratches on her hands and face—not to mention on the horses. But Marguerite was already looking at her suspiciously.

"Come on," she said. "You're not going to pull that safety warden thing this time, are you? Even you can't possibly come up with anything dangerous about following a trail. I mean, we can turn back if it gets too rough for the horses."

Lisa didn't have an answer for that. And she was starting to have the nagging feeling that maybe she was being a spoilsport. She would never agree to gallop horses on a winding trail no matter what, but she knew that if Carole or Stevie had suggested exploring a new trail, overgrown or not, Lisa would have agreed without hesitation.

"All right," she said reluctantly. "I guess the worst that can happen is we'll get lost. And the horses can find their way home if that happens."

"Whatever," Marguerite said, looking pleased. "Let's go!" She turned Amber and sent her plunging through the branches by the entrance to the trail.

Lisa sighed and followed.

". . . Then there's outcrossing. That's when two horses
are bred that are the same breed but come from totally
different lineages. And of course linebreeding. That's
sort of like inbreeding. It's where the same ancestor ap-
pears multiple times in a horse's family tree."

Tate was back. It was late afternoon, and Carole and
Stevie had finished with the grain and were visiting Calypso. Tate had found them there, and now all three of
them were discussing mare care. Fortunately Veronica
was nowhere in sight.

Stevie leaned on the half door of the stall. "Well, I
guess Max has done crossbreeding here, then," she said.
"Calypso is a Thoroughbred, and Geronimo's not. Judy
talked about that at the Horse Wise meeting."

"I wish I'd been there to hear the vet's lecture," Tate said. Stevie and Carole had already told him about Judy's talk the previous week. "I've read quite a bit about pregnant mares. But I'm sure it would have been interesting to hear about it with a live model standing right there."

"I know what you mean," Carole agreed. "Reading about things in books can be fun. But real-life experience is usually a lot better." She smiled at Tate. At first, she had been disappointed when Tate had left them to clean up the mess in the grain shed. But after discussing it, she and Stevie had agreed that they couldn't really blame him. Veronica had practically dragged him away, and besides, he hadn't made the mess—they had. Of course, if the situation had been reversed, Carole and Stevie would have helped him. But, after all, they were The Saddle Club. They made a habit of helping people.

Carole was still bothered by Tate's carelessness with the barley, but she tried to put it out of her mind. Stevie had been careless there, too, since she hadn't stopped him. Anyone could make a mistake, and no real harm had come of it this time. So why make a big deal of it?

Stevie was smiling at Tate. "So when are you going to join our riding class?" she asked him. "We were sure we'd see you today. You missed a fun time at Horse Wise."

"I'm sure I'll join soon," Tate replied, reaching to pull a stray piece of straw out of Calypso's mane. "Like I said,

78

I've had a few private lessons this week with Max. He just wants to make sure I'm up to speed before I join the group."

"Don't worry about that," Stevie said quickly. "If you're having any trouble, I'm sure Carole can help you catch up. She's the best rider in our class, and she loves to help out. Isn't that right, Carole?"

Carole smiled weakly. "I'm sure we'd all be willing to help," she said. Although somehow, she didn't think Tate would need much help. He knew more about horses than anybody she could think of, except maybe Max and Judy.

"Hello there, everyone!" came a cheerful voice behind them.

Carole turned. "Oh, hi, Simon," she said. "What are you still doing here? Jump class ended hours ago."

"I just finished doing some chores," Simon replied, walking over to the stall door and peering in. "And now I was just coming by to check on Calypso. You know, make sure she isn't going into labor or anything."

Tate gave him a look of disbelief. "Into labor?" he repeated. "Don't be ridiculous. She hasn't bagged up or anything. She hasn't shown any signs."

Simon seemed startled at the other boy's harsh tone. "Oh, um, I know," he said uncertainly. "I mean, I was sort of kidding. I just wanted to look in on her, that's all. I promised I would help watch her."

"Well, that won't do much good if you don't know

79

what you're watching for," Tate replied. He turned his back on the other boy and patted the mare on the neck.

Simon looked crestfallen. "I just wanted to help," he said quietly.

"Don't worry, Simon," Carole said, shooting Tate a perplexed look. "I'm sure Calypso appreciates it." She couldn't understand why Tate was being so hard on him.

"Right," Stevie put in. "Even if certain other people don't."

"Um, okay," Simon said. "Well, I'd better go." He slunk away before the girls could say another word.

Tate glanced at the two girls. Then he frowned. "Oops," he said. "Let me guess. You two think I was too rough on that guy."

Stevie put her hands on her hips. "No kidding," she said. "Everybody knows Simon is clueless, but you didn't have to be mean about it, Tate."

"I'm sorry," Tate said quickly. "I wasn't trying to be mean. Really." He sighed. "Sometimes I just get too impatient with people when they don't know what they're talking about, you know? It's a bad habit of mine. I can't help myself."

Carole thought about that for a second. She supposed that what Tate was saying made sense, sort of. It could be frustrating to know so much and have to deal with someone who didn't know anything at all. And Simon *did* take some getting used to. Maybe Tate hadn't responded the same way Carole herself would have, but why should he? They were two very different people, despite Stevie's claims to the contrary. Still . . .

Tate was biting his lip, looking anxious. "Maybe I should go find that Simon guy and apologize," he said. "What do you think?"

Stevie caught Carole's eye. Carole could tell that her friend was having the same kinds of thoughts she was. "Uh, I guess it's okay," Stevie told Tate. "Simon has probably forgotten about it already. He doesn't hold a grudge."

Carole nodded uncertainly. Suddenly she thought of something, and her eyes widened. She had just figured out another reason why Tate might have responded to Simon the way he had. Maybe he was jealous! After all, both boys were very good-looking, a fact that she was sure Tate was aware of even if Simon wasn't. Maybe Tate was feeling competitive about that and was trying to prove his superiority the only way he knew how—by showing off his knowledge about horses.

Carole was so excited about her theory that she almost blurted it out right then and there. But she bit her tongue. Saying anything about it would embarrass Tate—not to mention herself. But she couldn't wait to tell Stevie later.

LISA HAD BEEN growing steadily more nervous for the past twenty minutes. She and Marguerite were deep in the woods, and Lisa had completely lost her sense of direction. The path they had been following had twisted and turned and branched off so many times that she wasn't sure they would be able to find their way back. It was hard to see what was happening with the clouds because of the thick canopy of trees, but the chilly breeze snaking through the forest told Lisa that rain was probably coming soon. And by now she knew that they were a lot more than a ten-minute ride from the shelter of the stable.

Besides all that, she was getting heartily sick of Marguerite. The girl was shallower, stupider, and even less responsible than Lisa had originally thought. Ever since they had started following this trail, Marguerite had been babbling on and on about her friends and their parents and their houses and their purebred horses. Lisa was starting to suspect that those friends were the only reason Marguerite rode at all. She certainly didn't seem to have any real interest in horses or riding. Every time Lisa tried to change the subject to something horse-related, Marguerite found a way to change it back. It had turned into a sort of battle.

"So where do you think we are?" Lisa asked nervously. "Does Fox Crest's land extend this far, or do you think we're in the state park by now?"

Marguerite shrugged and pushed aside a branch that was in her way. "Who knows?" she said. "And what difference does it make, anyway?"

Lisa didn't answer. She was too busy catching the

branch that Marguerite had just carelessly released. "It's getting kind of late," she said instead. "Maybe we should—"

Marguerite's cry of delight interrupted her. "Wow! Look up there!"

Lisa urged Tiny forward until the big gray mare was shoulder to shoulder with Amber, and looked in the direction Marguerite was pointing.

They were approaching a different kind of landscape than the thickly growing trees and rambling underbrush that had surrounded their path up until now. Ahead, the trees thinned out to several yards apart. Grass and wildflowers, rather than thorns and shrubs, sprouted around them.

"Wow," Lisa said. "Someone must have cleared it out. It looks like a town park or something."

Marguerite nodded. "Come on, let's go."

"Wait." Lisa put out a hand to stop her. Marguerite paused and looked at her questioningly. "Look, Marguerite," Lisa said. "This has been a nice ride and everything. But I have a bus to catch. We really ought to start heading back now. It's going to pour any second, and it will take us a while to find our way—"

Marguerite was scowling. "What's your problem, Lisa?" she snapped. "You're such a total wet blanket! Don't you have any sense of adventure?"

Lisa frowned. That stung a little. Sure, she was more cautious than Marguerite was. That made her a good, safe rider, not some kind of old fuddy-duddy, the way the other girl was making it sound.

"I have a sense of adventure," she said sharply. "But I also have *common* sense. Something you might not have heard of."

Marguerite rolled her eyes. "Okay, now you're really starting to sound like my mother," she said, shortening her reins. "Look, I don't care what you do. I'm going to go check out the landscape up there." She tossed her head defiantly. "In fact, I think I'll try galloping in and out around those trees. Sort of like an obstacle course. It'll be fun. But I guess you wouldn't know anything about that."

Lisa gasped. "Are you crazy?" She couldn't believe that Marguerite was serious. "Amber isn't a barrel racer, you know. All it would take is one misstep or one exposed tree root and—"

Marguerite interrupted again. "Look, I've had enough of your lectures," she said. "Are you coming with me or not?"

"No way," Lisa said. "And you shouldn't go, either. Let's just head back."

"Forget it." Marguerite clucked to Amber, and the mare started forward eagerly. "You can go back if you want to. In fact, be my guest. Go get on your stupid bus and go back to Willow Creek."

"Fine!" Lisa exclaimed, exasperated. "Maybe I will!"

"Good," Marguerite replied with a smirk. "Have a nice life!" With that, she urged Amber into a trot, then a canter. The mare burst through the last few yards of underbrush, then broke into a gallop as she entered the parklike area. Lisa shouted after them, but it didn't do any good. Within seconds, Marguerite and her horse were out of sight.

Lisa's heart was pounding with fear. Not for herself—for Amber. The beautiful bay could be badly injured with such an irresponsible rider on her back.

Still, there was no way Lisa was going to risk Tiny's safety—and her own—by trying to catch Marguerite. "There's just one thing to do, old girl," she told Tiny. "We'd better get back to the stable as quickly as we can and tell someone what Marguerite is up to."

Tiny snorted and bobbed her head, seeming to agree. Then, as Lisa clucked to her and gave her her head, the gray mare moved forward into the parkland and then turned to one side, picking her way carefully between the trees at a walk.

Lisa sighed and tried not to worry too much about all the terrible things that could happen to Marguerite and her horse. She wasn't normally a tattletale, but this time she knew she had no choice. She had seen a few bad spills in her day. Recently, even Max had been seriously injured in a fall. She knew that accidents could happen to the best of riders. But she also knew they were much more likely to happen to those who were careless or reckless, and Marguerite definitely qualified on both counts.

A drop of rain splashed onto Tiny's mane, and Lisa groaned. "It figures," she muttered. If it had started raining five minutes earlier, maybe she could have convinced Marguerite to turn back with her.

Tiny was still moving steadily through the forest. Lisa knew that horses had an innate sense of direction that would lead them home. She also knew that Tiny wouldn't necessarily pick the same path back as the one they had followed to get there. She wasn't worried about that, but she was still worrying about Marguerite's foolhardy behavior. In fact, the more she thought about it, the more upset she got.

Tiny continued making her way through the woods. Lisa left the reins loose, letting the horse choose her own pace and her own path. The wind had picked up, and the rain was falling now in slow, oversized drops. Lisa hardly noticed. She clenched her teeth angrily as she remembered all the dangerous games Marguerite had wanted to play. Didn't she realize how stupid she was being? Riding was a fun sport, but you had to take it seriously if you wanted to do it well and safely. You couldn't just do whatever you felt like and forget about everything else.

The rain was starting to fall more heavily now. Lisa's hard hat was keeping the rain out of her face, though, so she didn't worry about it too much. However, she did glance down to make sure the ground wasn't getting muddy or rocky. She saw that Tiny was taking them down a broad, sloping hill studded with trees and thickly carpeted with grass and moss.

See? Lisa thought. *Marguerite never would have thought to check for mud and rocks. She never would have considered that her horse could fall because of this rain. She probably would have just gone galloping through it!*

That thought made Lisa madder than ever. She still couldn't believe that Marguerite had gone riding off by herself like that, never realizing that she could be putting herself and Amber in danger. Not to mention Lisa—

She never finished the thought. At that moment, Tiny stumbled and started to slide downhill. Lisa was jerked to one side, and her feet flew out of the stirrups. Too late, she realized that the hill had gotten a lot steeper since she had checked it just a moment before. She also suddenly remembered that grass and moss could be at least as slippery as mud when they were wet.

Tiny neighed fearfully and scrabbled at the slippery ground, trying to regain her balance. Her hindquarters slid to one side and she jerked wildly, trying to stay upright.

Lisa had stopped thinking about Marguerite now. Her only thought was staying in the saddle—and praying that Tiny didn't fall and crush her. She grabbed at Tiny's mane with both hands and gripped the mare's sides with her legs. But the horse's mane was slippery, and Lisa's left hand lost its grip. At the same time, Tiny whinnied and tossed her head.

That was all it took. Lisa was flung to the side, and the mane slipped out of her right hand. She hit the ground hard and slid downhill, unable to catch herself on the slick, steep, grassy ground. She came to an abrupt stop when she slammed into a large, solid tree that had suddenly loomed in front of her.

"Ow!" she cried as pain shot through her left arm, which had gotten caught between her body and the tree. A second later she felt a deeper, throbbing pain traveling down her back, and she squeezed her eyes shut and groaned as she waited for it to pass.

It didn't pass, but after a moment it subsided a little, and she forced herself to open her eyes and look around. She was wedged against a tree trunk halfway down the steep hill. A few yards below, she could see Tiny. She could hear her, too. The gray mare was whinnying loudly and tossing her head as she stood at the bottom of the hill. Fortunately, she was standing squarely on all four feet—that meant that she probably hadn't been injured in her wild slide.

"Thank goodness," Lisa whispered. But she knew she didn't have any time to waste. Tiny was obviously jittery. Lisa had to catch her before she panicked and ran off.

She tried to move, to push herself away from the tree

trunk, but the moment she lifted her left arm, she could tell that there was something wrong with her wrist. And when she tried to sit up, the pain flamed out from her spine again. Her head spun crazily, and for a second she thought she was going to pass out.

Her head cleared quickly. "Wow," she muttered. She pushed her damp hair out of her eyes with her right hand, then tried again, moving herself more carefully this time. Every motion brought stabs of pain—to her wrist, to her back, and then to her left ankle as well.

She managed to drag herself to a sitting position, with her good leg wedged against the tree trunk. Her back felt as if it were on fire, but Lisa did her best to ignore the pain. She also ignored the rain, which was now coming down in wild, windblown spurts, and gazed down the hill at Tiny. The mare was standing still, but she kept jerking her head from side to side and snorting loudly, her eyes rolling with fear.

"Tiny!" Lisa called. She was surprised at how weak and shaky her voice sounded. Tiny hadn't even heard her. She cleared her throat and prepared to try again.

At that moment, a thunderclap exploded somewhere in the near distance. That was all the nervous mare could take. Tiny threw up her head, neighed shrilly in terror, and took off at a run, leaving Lisa all alone.

7

LISA FELT READY to panic, too. Her situation kept getting worse. The skies had opened up with the thunderclap, and it was really pouring now. Her ankle and wrist were throbbing, and her back screamed in protest every time she tried to move.

With an effort of will, she shoved herself away from the tree trunk, feet first. She slid over the grass, trying to slow her progress with her good arm, and managed to make it to the bottom of the hill without injuring herself any further.

Once she was on flat ground again, she sat up gingerly and tried to decide what to do. Her first thought was to try to walk, or at least limp. But after attempting to climb to her feet, she knew it was hopeless. Even if she could have put some weight on her injured ankle—or found a branch to use as a cane—the pain in her back was too severe to let her take more than a step or two.

She collapsed flat on the ground on her stomach, squeezing her eyes shut tight as she waited for the shooting pains to subside again. What was she going to do? She was in a strange forest, far from any traveled trail, in the middle of a rainstorm. She couldn't walk, and even if she could, she wouldn't know which way to go. She buried her face in her uninjured arm and started to cry.

She was sobbing so loudly that she almost didn't hear the sound coming from directly above her. A soft, tentative sound, almost lost in the pounding of the rain and the whistling of the wind through the treetops. A familiar sound. Lisa stopped crying. Could it be?

Gathering all her strength, she rolled onto her side and looked up. A pair of large, soft brown eyes stared back at her. Then the sound came again: a whuffling nicker.

"Tiny!" Lisa cried. "You came back!" She started to sit up quickly but remembered her injured back just in time. Taking it slowly, she managed to ease herself up into a sitting position without setting off a new round of agony.

Tiny watched her all the while. Lisa wasn't sure, but she thought the mare looked worried and a little sheepish.

"Don't worry about it, girl," Lisa said through

clenched teeth as she carefully drew her legs up under her. "I don't blame you for getting scared. But I have to tell you"—she groaned as her weight landed on her injured ankle—"I don't think I've ever been so glad to see a horse in my entire life!"

Tiny whickered again and lowered her big head to snuffle at Lisa, accidentally knocking off her hard hat in the process. Another boom of thunder rang out in the distance, but this time Tiny didn't even flinch.

Lisa couldn't help smiling, despite her pain. Suddenly things were looking a little better. She didn't think she could ride, but maybe if she leaned on Tiny, she could hop back to civilization. . . .

It didn't take long for her to figure out that that wasn't going to work, either. She managed to pull herself to a standing position by grabbing one of Tiny's dangling stirrups. The mare seemed to understand what to do, moving forward slowly, step by careful step, at Lisa's urging. But even keeping her weight off her injured leg wasn't enough. The pain in Lisa's back got worse and worse with every movement. She only managed to make it as far as the base of a large tree trunk before she had to stop, leaning all her weight on Tiny's strong shoulder.

"Okay, so much for that idea," Lisa moaned. She knew she wasn't going to be able to make it all the way back to the stable at this rate, no matter how patient and strong Tiny was. "Oh, Tiny!" she cried. "What am I going to do?" She wrapped her arms around the mare's huge, solid neck and buried her face in her mane.

STEVIE WAS AT Calypso's stall again. Carole still wasn't back from mucking out Starlight's stall.

Stevie glanced at her watch, wondering if Carole had gotten caught up in something else and forgotten the time. But before she could really start to worry, Carole appeared around the corner of the aisle, panting and breathless.

"Whew!" she exclaimed, hurrying to join Stevie. "You'll never believe what I was just doing."

"Hmmm?" As soon as she had seen Carole coming, Stevie had returned her attention to Calypso, who was moving about restlessly in her stall. "Look, she's pacing," she said worriedly. "Do you think that's a sign the foal is coming?"

Carole gave the mare a quick look. "I don't think so," she said. "She wasn't showing any other signs when we checked her earlier. She probably just wants to stretch her legs."

Stevie nodded, satisfied. That was what she had thought, too. Now that Carole agreed, she was certain. "What were you saying?"

"Huh?" Carole was still staring at Calypso. "Oh. I said, you'll never believe what I was doing just now. I was cleaning Tate's tack!"

"Really?" Stevie said. "Did he ask you for help?"

Carole frowned. "Not exactly."

"Well?" Stevie asked. Her eyes widened. "Oh! Did you finally get to see him ride? How was he? Is he really great? Which horse was he—"

"Stevie!" Carole said sharply.

Stevie shut up and gave Carole an inquisitive look.

"I didn't see him ride," Carole said, leaning against the wall. "I haven't seen him since we were all here earlier. I guess Red was working with him in the indoor ring while we were helping Max stack those bales in the hayloft."

Stevie looked disappointed. Then she looked puzzled. "So how did you end up cleaning his tack?"

"I found it in the tack room," Carole said. "He had just left it there all sweaty."

"How do you know it was his?"

"Mrs. Reg told me." Mrs. Reg was Max's mother. She helped Max run the stable, and she could always find a job for idle hands. Carole shrugged. "She asked me to help out and clean it, so of course I did. Can you believe he just left it there?"

Calypso had stopped pacing and come over to the door, and Stevie ran her fingers through the horse's mane. "That's kind of weird," she said slowly. "Maybe he didn't realize he was supposed to clean his own tack after he rode."

94

"Maybe." Carole sighed. "Actually, that's what I kept telling myself. Maybe Tate's old stable was the kind of place where the stable hands do all the work and the riders just ride."

Stevie nodded. "The kind of place where the instructors don't care as much about their riders practicing all the different things that go into horse care." She was sure that was the explanation for Tate's behavior—all of Tate's behavior. He was still adjusting to Pine Hollow.

Stevie was starting to believe that Tate wasn't as perfect as she had first thought. Still, that was no surprise, was it? No boy was perfect—even Phil had a tiny flaw or two if you got right down to it. That didn't change Stevie's opinion that Tate had definite potential as a boyfriend for Carole. After all, wasn't he just as horse-crazy as she was? Didn't he know even more than she did about everything there was to know about horses? And wasn't he absolutely adorable?

Carole had opened the door of Calypso's stall and was patting the mare on the neck. "She's definitely restless," she announced. "Maybe we should take her for a walk outside."

Stevie raised an eyebrow, then glanced up at the roof. The sound of rain pounding steadily against it had been going on for at least half an hour. "Um, Carole?" she said. "I'm not sure that's such a good idea."

"What do you mean?" Carole asked in surprise. "Judy said it was safe to walk her, and I really think . . ." Her voice trailed off as she noticed Stevie's finger pointing upward. She grinned sheepishly. "Oh. It's raining."

Stevie reached for Calypso's halter. "How about a little stroll around the indoor ring instead?"

"Sounds good," Carole agreed.

A few minutes later the two girls were walking around the ring with the pregnant mare in tow. Stevie filled Carole in on what she had just been thinking about Tate.

"I know what you mean," Carole said when she had finished. "Tate's still new here, and we really should give him the benefit of the doubt." She blushed and looked at her feet. "Besides," she mumbled, "he really is awfully good-looking, isn't he?"

Stevie grinned. "Let the record show: Ms. Carole Hanson actually admitted that a boy was cute!"

"Good-looking!" Carole protested, laughing. "That's different from cute."

Stevie smirked. "Oh, really?"

"Yes, really," Carole said firmly. "Definitely different."

They walked around the ring quietly for a few minutes, each of them thinking her own thoughts. Calypso walked slowly along with them, her rounded belly swaying gently from side to side. The rain continued to patter rhythmically on the roof.

96

Carole was the first to break the silence. "This is really cozy, isn't it?"

"There's only one thing that would make it absolutely perfect," Stevie said.

"I know." Carole nodded. "If only Lisa were here with us."

It was cold and the rain was falling harder. Lisa had hoped that after a few minutes of rest she would feel up to moving, maybe even riding. But she was beginning to realize that neither was going to be an option anytime soon—especially the riding part. She had dragged herself to her feet with Tiny's stirrup again, and now she was leaning against the tree trunk, trying to figure out what to do. Her wrist throbbed. Her back ached. And her ankle felt numb. She thought it was starting to swell. The tree offered her a little protection from the rain, but not much. She tried to take a step away from the tree and almost collapsed before she grabbed for the trunk again.

"Well, that little experiment didn't work, did it, Tiny?" she said bleakly.

The mare snorted and nuzzled her, almost knocking her off her feet.

"You're right." Lisa gave a rueful smile. "I guess I might as well sit down. I'm sure not going anywhere right now."

Still holding on to the tree, she carefully lowered herself to a sitting position. That hurt almost as much as standing, but the ground was wet and she really didn't want to lie down. Besides, that would feel too much like giving up.

She wrapped her arms around herself, being careful not to further injure her left wrist. The wind was getting stronger, blowing the rain straight through the sparse spring leaves in the treetops. Lisa shivered from the cold, and her skin felt clammy. She guessed that she was probably in a mild state of shock from the fall. She tried to remember what she was supposed to do about that—something about elevating her feet. Or was it her head?

Either way, Lisa decided it wasn't going to happen. She had all she could do to stay calm and try to come up with a plan. Now, if she could just focus . . .

It was no good. Her brain didn't seem to be working. And she was so cold. . . . "Oh, Tiny," she cried, shivering violently despite her warm sweater. "I can't walk. I can't ride. I can hardly move. And nobody even knows I'm out here!"

The truth of the last statement suddenly struck her. Marguerite thought that Lisa had gone straight back to the stable and then home on the bus. Maybe she would notice that Tiny was missing, realize what must have happened, and send help. Then again, maybe not. After all, Tiny's stall was tucked away in the back of the stable somewhere. If Marguerite didn't bother to check on the big gray horse—which she almost certainly wouldn't—there was no telling how long it would be until Tiny was missed. It might not be until the grooms started the evening feeding. When would that be?

Lisa glanced at her watch. The glass was gone, and the face was mangled and unreadable. She realized that the watch, like her wrist, had smashed into the tree trunk in her fall.

Lisa squeezed her eyes shut, trying to keep the rain out and the tears in. After a moment, she heard a snuffling, grunting sound. She opened her eyes and saw that Tiny was slowly, ponderously lowering herself to the ground nearby. Lisa watched in amazement as the mare tucked her front legs to one side and wiggled her hindquarters, making herself comfortable on the wet grass.

"Tiny?" Lisa whispered.

She moved toward the horse, doing her best not to aggravate her injuries. Soon she was close enough to lean back carefully against Tiny's broad, strong shoulder.

The mare's skin felt soft and warm. Lisa wiped most of the moisture off the saddle and leaned back farther, allowing her body to relax.

Tiny turned her head and sniffed at Lisa's hair. Then she let out a soft, horsey sigh and let her eyelids droop. Lisa let her eyes close partway, too, enjoying the warmth and comfort of the big body supporting her.

"SO YOU'RE EXCITED about this," Stevie said, her eyes glowing. "Right? Right?"

Carole bit her lip. She glanced at Starlight, who was standing patiently in cross-ties as the two girls groomed him. Then she grinned. "Well—let's not say excited," she said. "How about just sort of interested?"

"That's good enough for me!" Stevie grinned back. She was feeling extremely proud of herself. She had just managed to do the one thing she had been plotting for the last week: set up a date for Carole and Tate.

Okay, Stevie admitted to herself as she ran a body brush down Starlight's side, *so technically maybe it wasn't exactly a date.* All she had done was invite Tate to join The Saddle Club at TD's in a little while. But it was a start.

"This will give you and Tate a chance to really get to know each other," Stevie said with satisfaction. "Away from all the distractions of the stable—including a certain Veronica diAngelo."

Carole looked up from working a knot out of Starlight's mane. "Are you sure he really wanted to come?" She wasn't sure how she felt about all this. One part of her kept remembering the things about Tate that bothered her, like when he'd left his tack uncleaned or when he was snippy with Simon. But another part of her couldn't wait to talk to him more about horses and find out just how much he really knew. The more she heard him talk, the more impressed she was with the depth of his knowledge. Was being in awe the same as liking someone?

"Of course he wanted to come," Stevie said, sounding a little impatient. "He's crazy about you. I have a sixth sense about these things, trust me. And who can blame him? You two are perfect for each other."

"Well, I don't know about that," Carole said slowly, dropping the comb she'd been using into Starlight's grooming bucket.

Stevie shrugged. "I know what you're thinking," she said. "And you don't have to worry. Tate may be a little rough around the edges—what guy isn't?—but he knows horses. That's the important thing, right?"

"I guess so." Carole decided not to worry about it anymore. It wasn't as if it were a real date. After all, Stevie and Lisa would be there, too. She gave Starlight a pat. "I think we're just about finished here. Should we put him away and then go check on Calypso one more time?"

Stevie tossed the body brush into the bucket. "Sounds good to me," she said. "We don't need to leave to meet Lisa for half an hour or so. Let's go."

The two girls were walking down the aisle toward Calypso's stall a few minutes later when they heard excited voices coming from around the corner. Stevie stopped in her tracks when she recognized Veronica's voice. "What's she still doing here?" she muttered. She had hoped the other girl had finally gone home and left Tate in peace.

". . . Anyway, he's totally adorable, don't you think?" Veronica was saying, sounding very pleased with herself as usual. "We'll make a perfect couple."

There was an answering giggle; then someone said, "Totally! You're perfect for each other."

"That's Betsy Cavanaugh," Carole whispered. Betsy was in their riding class and was a friend of Veronica's.

Stevie put a finger to her lips and leaned forward to listen again.

"I know," Veronica was saying, sounding more self-satisfied than ever. "So I just heard Max and Red talking. They're both going to be working with Tate in a few minutes. I guess he's so talented that he needs two instructors."

"Awesome," Betsy said.

"Uh-huh," Veronica said smugly. "And I'm definitely going to be there to watch."

Stevie had heard all she needed to hear. She tiptoed away from the corner, gesturing for Carole to follow.

"Did you hear that?" she demanded grimly.

Carole nodded. "I heard it. What do we do now?"

"We can't let her mess up our plan. We're so close!" Stevie paced back and forth, frowning thoughtfully. Suddenly she stopped and snapped her fingers. "Of course!" she said. "It's so simple. We beat her at her own game."

Carole wasn't sure she liked the sound of that. "What do you mean?" she asked cautiously.

Stevie was grinning now. "I mean *you* should be the one to show up for Tate's private lesson, not Veronica."

"But we don't even know where the lesson is," Carole protested.

"Of course we do." Stevie pointed up at the roof. Rain was still drumming down on it. "It's in the indoor ring. Where else?"

Carole grinned. "And I thought Lisa was the logical one," she teased. Her grin faded. "But Veronica—"

"Leave her to me," Stevie said firmly. She grabbed Carole by the arm and dragged her down the aisle toward the indoor ring. "You just get in there."

"Wait." Carole yanked her arm away and stopped. "We can't go. We have to check on Calypso before we leave for TD's."

Stevie sighed but didn't argue. Instead, she glanced around the aisle. Voices were coming from a nearby stall.

"That sounds like Britt," she said, listening carefully. "And Polly." She hurried toward the stall.

Minutes later, it was settled. The other two girls promised to look in on Calypso, and Stevie was once again dragging Carole down the aisle.

This time Carole didn't resist. She and Stevie almost collided with Veronica in the open area just outside the entrance to the indoor ring.

Veronica frowned when she saw them. "What are you two doing here?" she asked in a nasty tone of voice.

"Looking for you," Stevie said smoothly. She dropped Carole's arm and took Veronica's instead. "Um, you have a phone call. In Mrs. Reg's office."

Veronica looked suspicious. She glanced from Stevie to the door of the indoor ring and back again. "What are you talking about?"

Stevie smiled innocently. "A phone call," she said. She decided to take a wild guess. "Um, I think it's your tailor. Something about your new designer riding jacket being lost in a terrible tailor shop fire—"

"What!" Veronica exclaimed. "Get out of my way! I've got to get to that phone!" She shoved past Stevie and rushed down a nearby hallway toward Mrs. Reg's office.

Stevie grinned. She hadn't known that Veronica was having a designer jacket made. It had just been a hunch. But it went to show exactly how predictable Veronica really was.

"Okay," Stevie told Carole cheerfully, gesturing toward the door. "He's all yours. I'll guard the door in case she comes back."

Carole gulped and glanced at the door. She could hear voices coming from behind it; the lesson must have already started. "Okay," she said. "Wish me luck!"

9

RAIN DRIPPED DOWN Lisa's face, mixing with her tears. She was getting desperate. She had no idea how much time had passed since her fall. It didn't help that she thought she might have dozed off for a while, leaning against Tiny. But in any case, she was sure that she had been out there for a long time. It wasn't dark, but she knew it would be soon. Marguerite hadn't returned yet, which meant that she hadn't noticed anything was wrong.

That meant Lisa wouldn't be missed until Tiny's dinnertime. Or maybe even until her parents got home to Willow Creek and found out she wasn't there.

Lisa knew she couldn't lie there that long. Even the warmth of Tiny's big body couldn't keep her warm all night. At least the rain had slowed. There was just a faint drizzle now, working its way through the leaves.

"Okay, Tiny," Lisa said. Her voice came out in a croak, and she cleared her throat. "Okay," she said again. "It's time to take some action."

She had to try to move again, no matter how much it hurt. That was all there was to it. There was a large, jagged rock nearby. If she could step up onto that, she could mount Tiny. And once she was in the saddle, as long as she kept the big mare to a gentle walk, she *would* ride.

"Come on, girl," Lisa said. "Time to get up." She pushed herself away from the horse's side. Her muscles screamed in protest, along with her injured back and leg. She had been lying in the same position for so long that even her uninjured limbs were stiff.

Ignoring that, she sat up as straight as she could, resting her weight on her right hand. By pushing with her right leg, she got herself into a crawling position. Then she paused for breath.

Tiny had been watching closely. She let out a tremendous snort and lurched quickly to her feet. She stepped over to Lisa and put down her head to examine the girl's face.

Lisa couldn't help smiling as she felt the mare's hot breath on her forehead. "Good girl, Tiny," she gasped. She crawled carefully over to the rock, trying not to notice the hammering pain in her back or the sweat breaking out on her forehead.

When she reached the rock, Lisa whistled for Tiny. The horse came to her immediately, and Lisa once again hauled herself up by the stirrup.

"Boy, am I glad I tightened that girth nice and snug," she muttered.

Soon she was standing—sort of. She leaned heavily against Tiny, still keeping a firm grip on the saddle with her good hand. Then she cautiously lifted her injured leg onto the top of the rock and gingerly put some weight on it. It almost buckled beneath her, but Lisa gritted her teeth and continued.

A few long, painful minutes later, she was on top of the rock, leaning against the saddle. Lisa knew that she wasn't going to be able to mount in the usual way, from the left side of the horse. Her left foot wouldn't support her weight while she swung her right foot over.

When she thought about that, tears of frustration welled up in her eyes again. This was ridiculous. Even if she turned the mare around and tried to mount from the right, there was no way she could do it. Her back hurt when she sat up or turned her head. How was she going to get into the saddle—and stay there?

She collapsed against the saddle in despair. Tiny turned her head to see what she was doing, whickering quizzically.

"Oh, Tiny," Lisa said. "This is hopeless." She looked around. From her new, slightly higher position atop the rock, she could see a little farther into the woods around her. A few yards away, on the other side of a slight rise, she spotted a small, tumbling stream, swollen with the rain.

Lisa gritted her teeth and made a vow. She was going to get to that stream. Then Tiny could take a drink, and Lisa could rinse off her sweaty face and maybe soak her sore wrist. She didn't know what would happen after that, but she decided not to think about it. The stream was her only goal.

She leaned more of her weight onto Tiny's back again, preparing herself for the jarring step down off the rock.

"Okay, Tiny," she muttered determinedly. "Here goes nothing."

STEVIE WAS STILL standing guard when Carole and Tate emerged from the indoor ring. Twenty minutes had passed, and except for one more encounter with Veronica, Stevie hadn't seen a soul. She had been tempted to peek inside and see how the lesson was going, but she hadn't let herself do it. She knew Carole would give her all the details later.

Carole had a funny look on her face when she came out. Stevie wasn't sure what it meant. Was Carole madly in love? Or had Tate been such a fantastic rider that she was jealous?

"Hi, guys," Stevie said brightly. "How was the lesson?"

"Great," Tate said with a grin. "Max let me ride a really cool horse today. His name's Patch."

Stevie was a little surprised. Patch was a very calm, steady horse. Usually Max only put new or nervous riders on the gentle gelding. Stevie would have expected Tate to ride one of the more spirited intermediate-level horses, maybe Barq or Comanche. Still, she figured Max had his reasons. He usually did.

Right now Stevie was a lot less interested in that than she was in figuring out what was up with Carole. She definitely looked strange. Besides, Stevie was dying to tell her how she had gotten rid of Veronica the second time. She had to figure out a way to get Carole alone before they all left for TD's.

Fortunately, Tate saved her the trouble. "Hey, I know we're supposed to leave soon for the ice cream place," he said. "Can I just call my folks and tell them? It will only take a minute."

"No problem," Stevie said quickly. "Take your time. I want to change out of my boots, anyway."

Tate headed for the pay phone, whistling cheerfully as he walked. Stevie grabbed Carole, who was still just standing there with that odd look on her face, and dragged her toward the student locker room.

"Boy, it's a good thing I stayed outside to guard the door," Stevie said as they entered. "Veronica came back after about five minutes, steaming mad because she figured out I made up that story. I practically had to block the door with my body to keep her from going in." She grinned proudly as she kicked her boots off and tossed them in the general direction of her cubby. "Then I started telling her about Tate. I told her how I'd been talking to him, and he said his family is really poor—*destitute* was the word I used, actually. I learned that one from Lisa. It means *really, really* poor."

"Really?" Carole said. She looked kind of distracted, and Stevie wasn't sure she was listening. "Um, Stevie—"

"That's not all," Stevie interrupted eagerly, waving one sneaker in the air. "It gets better. I knew that if I really wanted to turn her off, I had to make it worse than him just being poor. So I told her his father had been in jail and his mother raised chickens in the house, and—"

"Stevie!" Carole spoke more firmly this time. She glanced over at the doorway. "Listen to me for a second."

"What?" Stevie said. "I was just— Oh! I meant to ask you. How was the lesson? Are you madly in love?"

Carole took a deep breath. "Not quite," she said. "I—I just found out something kind of surprising."

Stevie looked up from tying her sneaker. Carole looked so serious that Stevie couldn't imagine what she was going to say next. "What is it?" she demanded.

Carole checked the door again, then leaned forward and lowered her voice. "Tate . . ." She paused and bit her lip. "Tate is a *horrible* rider!"

Stevie gasped and let her foot fall to the floor. "What do you mean?"

"I mean he's horrible," Carole said. "He's inconsiderate and heavy-handed, and he sits in the saddle like a sack of potatoes. He kept jerking poor Patch's head all around, and nothing Max and Red said seemed to make any difference." She shook her head. "Didn't you notice that he didn't have Patch with him when he came out? I'm pretty sure it's because Max didn't trust that he could cool a horse out properly. He offered to do it himself."

Stevie let out a low whistle. "Wow," she said. "Who would have guessed?"

"Not me," Carole said ruefully. "I was so impressed with all his knowledge that it never occurred to me he wouldn't be able to ride. You know what the worst part is? I don't think Tate even realizes how bad he is. He doesn't communicate with his horse at all."

Stevie bent to tie her other sneaker, thinking hard. "I guess this does explain a few things, though," she said slowly.

"You mean like why Tate never seemed to be interested in helping out with chores?" Carole nodded. "I thought of that, too."

"I guess all the horse knowledge in the world doesn't help if you don't have, um . . ." Stevie searched for the right word.

Carole guessed what she was thinking. "Real horse-craziness?" she said. "Or maybe I should say real horse *caring*. That could mean caring *about* horses . . ."

"And also caring *for* them," Stevie finished. She sighed and looked at Carole. "How did we miss seeing it sooner?"

Carole blushed. "I'm not sure," she said. "Partly, I guess we might have been giving him the benefit of the doubt because he's new. But also . . ."

Her voice trailed off, but Stevie nodded. "I know," she said. "We were dazzled by the way he looks." She rolled her eyes. "Remind me not to let a pretty face fool me next time, okay?" She glanced around the locker room. "Look, we've got to find a way to get out of bringing him to TD's."

Carole gasped. "I almost forgot about that!" she cried. "After what I just saw, I don't think I could sit across a table from him without throwing my sundae in his face."

Stevie jumped to her feet. "Come on, let's go to Calypso's stall," she said. "We should check on her before we leave anyway, and it might take him a few more minutes to track us down there. That should be enough time to come up with a plan."

BUT A FEW minutes later, they hadn't thought of a thing. Neither one of them wanted to be rude to Tate.

"After all, we did invite him," Carole said glumly, running her hand along Calypso's neck. The girls were

114

in the stall with the mare, who was quietly munching on a mouthful of hay.

"Thanks for saying *we*," Stevie said. She hadn't forgotten that it had been her idea to ask Tate to TD's. That made her more determined than ever to figure out a subtle, sneaky way to *un*invite him. "I still can't believe he can't ride. I mean, he knows so much. . . ."

"I know," Carole said. "Still, we've seen something like this before, you know."

"We have?" Stevie said in surprise. "When?"

Carole shrugged. "With Veronica, of course," she said. "I mean, she's a pretty good rider, but that's sort of the point. She rides well, and she has all the right clothes and equipment—"

"And then some," Stevie agreed. "But all that doesn't make her horse-crazy."

Carole grinned and nodded. "Just crazy."

Stevie didn't laugh. Her mouth had just dropped open, and she had an excited look in her eye. "I've got it!" she cried. "I just figured out how we can—"

"Aha, there you are," Tate said, poking his head into the stall. "I thought I might find you two in here. So, are you almost ready to go? I'm starving after all that riding. Some ice cream will really hit the spot." He rubbed his stomach and grinned.

"Sure," Stevie said quickly, before Carole could answer. "We're almost ready. Um, why don't you and Carole head outside now? I'll meet you there in a minute. I just remembered, I left something in the locker room."

Carole gave her a dismayed look. "Are you sure, Stevie?" she asked. "Uh, I think we ought to stay with Calypso. You never know when she might drop that foal."

Tate raised an eyebrow, looking surprised. "What are you talking about, Carole?" he said. "She's nowhere near ready yet. Anyone can see that."

Carole's face was turning red, but Stevie didn't have time to worry about that. "Just go ahead," she whispered as they left the stall. "Trust me."

Carole nodded and headed off with Tate without another word. Tate immediately started chattering about the signs of impending delivery in pregnant mares, and Carole turned and shot Stevie a look of pure despair.

Stevie gave her a thumbs-up sign. Then, as soon as Carole had turned away, Stevie crossed her fingers. She hoped this was going to work. . . .

LISA WAS TRYING to stay optimistic. It wasn't easy. The rain had finally stopped, but the clouds were still there, which was making dusk come faster than usual. She had reached the bank of the stream, but by the time she got there her entire body hurt so much that she could hardly stand it. At least she had been able to bathe her injured wrist in the chilly water. That had helped a little—

116

except it had made her back feel even worse by comparison.

Tiny had taken a long, deep drink from the stream. Then she had lowered herself to the ground beside Lisa once again. Lisa had almost cried when she did that. She could hardly imagine how much worse she would feel if she were out there all alone.

"Thanks for sticking by me, Tiny," she said, slinging her right arm over the mare's broad shoulders. "A lot of horses would have been so scared by the storm that they would have run straight back to the barn without looking back. But not you."

She stroked the horse's mane with her fingers, automatically starting to work at a tangled spot.

"Even if I can't ride you back," she went on, "it helps just to have you here, keeping me company." She let her fingers relax and rested her head against the warm gray neck. "I can't remember the last time a horse helped me so much." Suddenly she realized that wasn't really fair. "Well, actually, now that I think about it," she murmured thoughtfully, "other horses have helped me out quite a bit in the past. My friends, too."

She started stroking Tiny's mane again. The mare let out a sigh of contentment. It almost seemed as though Tiny liked listening to Lisa talk. Besides, talking to the horse made Lisa feel a little better, a little less panicky, so she continued.

"For instance," she said, "there's the horse I usually ride. Prancer is her name, and she's wonderful. She's helped me in so many ways—I guess the easiest to explain is the way she ran her heart out when I had to ride for help after Max's fall. . . ."

She shuddered at the memory. It was scary to remember how still Max had been out there on the steep, rocky trail of their endurance ride. She preferred to remember how brave Prancer had been, racing swiftly just as she had been bred to do—though not on a smooth, flat track, but over a rocky, wooded mountain trail after a long, long day of riding.

"She was wonderful that day," Lisa told Tiny, brushing a spot of drying mud off the horse's neck. "But she's helped me in less dramatic ways, too. One time I entered her in a horse show before either one of us was ready." She blushed at that memory. "I learned a lot from that, believe me.

"Then there was the horse I rode when I was on vacation on an island called San Marco. His name was Jasper, and he was kind of like you, Tiny—solid and steady. He helped me save a girl whose horse ran away with her." Lisa's leg was starting to throb again, but she ignored it and went on. "My friends have gotten a lot of help from horses, too. For instance, I know that riding and being around horses really helped Carole cope after her mother died." She paused. "Especially a horse named Cobalt. When Cobalt died, Carole was really upset, but I

118

think it helped her a lot when his son was born. That's Samson. Raising him and training him helped all of us in The Saddle Club learn a lot, too."

Lisa shifted carefully into a more comfortable position. Tiny's skin still felt warm and comforting under her arm.

"And if you want to talk about horses helping people," Lisa went on, "I know we're all really grateful to a brave pony named Maverick. He saved Carole's life when she was caught in a dangerous riptide. Then there's Stewball, the horse Stevie rides whenever we all visit our friends' ranch out West. He's a really interesting horse, and he's taken care of Stevie really well. Once he even helped show her how important it is for a rider to find exactly the right horse. Maybe that's how she ended up with Belle."

The light was fading faster now. Lisa tried not to think about that.

"And speaking of the ranch, our friend Kate has really been helped by her horse, Moonglow. Kate used to be a competitive rider, but for a while she didn't like riding much at all. Now she loves it again, and it's partly thanks to Moonglow—and a few other horses, too."

Now that she thought about it, Lisa realized that she and her friends really had gained just as much from riding and caring for horses as the horses had gained from them. Probably more.

"Then there are all the wonderful Pine Hollow horses,

of course," Lisa murmured. Her eyes were starting to feel heavy, but she didn't want to fall asleep. Once it got dark, it would be too easy for someone riding nearby to miss her unless she called out. "I already talked about Prancer. Another horse who helped me a lot was the horse I used to ride. His name was Pepper. He was a wonderful horse, and he taught me a lot. But eventually he got old and sick, and I was the one who had to decide to have Judy put him to sleep. It was the hardest thing I ever had to do, but it really helped me to be able to sit with him and say good-bye." Her eyes filled with tears at the memory. "And then there are so many other great horses, like Belle and Starlight— oh, and of course Topside. He's one of Max's best horses, and Stevie used to ride him before she got Belle. Topside once helped our friend Skye Ransom—he's a movie star."

Lisa paused. For just a second, she felt silly telling Tiny all this. What did a horse know or care about movie stars or any of the rest of it?

But Lisa decided not to worry about that. She was sure that somehow, in her own way, Tiny was listening and understanding—if not the exact meaning of the words, then some part of what Lisa was telling her.

"Anyway, Skye rode Topside in one of his movies, and it kind of saved the day because the horse Skye had been riding wouldn't behave, and . . . well, you get the gist of it. Topside basically saved Skye's whole career." Suddenly Lisa remembered something even more important

120

that Topside had done. "Also, one time when Stevie took Topside to riding camp, the two of them helped save a whole lot of horses when the barn caught on fire."

She was definitely feeling sleepy now, so she took a deep breath and opened her eyes as wide as she could. "And of course," she told Tiny, "I haven't even started to tell you about how horses helped get Max together with his wife, Deborah. . . ."

"PLEASE LET HER still be here, please let her still be here, please let her still be here," Stevie muttered as she hurried down the aisles at Pine Hollow. She was looking for someone who was usually the last person on earth she wanted to see.

She rounded a corner and spotted that someone standing in the aisle. Someone wearing a pair of fancy riding breeches and a silky, expensive-looking shirt.

"Veronica!" Stevie cried happily. "There you are."

Veronica looked surprised at the greeting. She also looked suspicious. "What do you want?" she demanded, backing away from her horse's stall and crossing her arms across her chest. "Are you here to tell me more about how Lisa saw Tate picking his nose in math class?"

Stevie grinned. That had been one of the high points of her earlier Tate stories. Then her grin faded and she gulped as she realized what she had to do now.

"Um, actually I might have been exaggerating about that a little," she said, kicking at a stray clump of straw in the stable aisle.

"Yeah, right." Veronica rolled her eyes. "Like I hadn't figured that out already. I bet none of that stuff you said is true. You were just trying to make him sound bad so nobody would want to hang out with him but you and your loser friends." She smirked. "And just to make sure of that, I'm going to ask Tate about all that stuff myself. Just so I can make absolutely sure of what I already know—that you're a big fat liar."

For a second, Stevie was annoyed. She had thought her earlier stories had been pretty convincing. How dare Veronica accuse her of lying!

But then she realized that this was actually good news. It meant that her task was going to be a lot easier than she'd thought.

"Well, go ahead and ask him if you want," she said casually. "But you'll have to wait until tomorrow. You see, right now Tate is coming to TD's with The Saddle Club. So you'll just have to wait your turn to hear the *real* story of Tate's life—like how his great-great-uncle twice removed is second cousin to the Queen of England, and how Tate's grandfather helped build the Washington Monument—"

"TD's?" Veronica interrupted, a crafty look crossing her face for a second. "Oh, well, hmmm. That's too bad. I'll catch him tomorrow, I guess." She whirled and hurried down the aisle without another word.

Stevie paused to give Veronica's horse, Danny, a pat on the nose. "Did anyone ever tell you your owner is a sucker?" she said with a grin.

HALF AN HOUR later, Carole wasn't sure whom she felt sorrier for—Tate or Veronica. She had no idea how Stevie had arranged things. All she knew was that she, Stevie, and Tate had hardly made themselves comfortable in one of the booths at the ice cream shop before the little bell above the door rang and Veronica rushed in. She'd invited herself to join them, and ever since, she and Tate had been doing their best to impress each other.

"Yes, I know all about foxhunting," Veronica was saying to Tate. She seemed to have forgotten that Stevie and Carole were at the table. "After all, my family is rather socially prominent, if I do say so myself."

"She does," Stevie whispered behind her napkin to Carole. "And she did."

Veronica didn't hear her. "Yes, we have quite a reputation in this town. Did you know that four out of five people in Willow Creek owe money to my father's bank?"

"Hmmm," Tate said, dipping his spoon into his sundae. "Interesting. Did you know that most horses can't stand pigs?"

Carole rolled her eyes. "How much longer do you think this will go on?" she murmured, leaning toward Stevie.

Stevie shrugged and grinned. "Who knows?" she said. "I just hope Lisa gets here in time to witness the fun." She glanced at the clock on the wall. "I wonder what's keeping her, anyway."

LISA WASN'T HAVING any fun at all. It was getting darker and chillier with each passing minute, and it had started raining again. Her leg was throbbing more than ever. She couldn't move it much anymore. And there was still no sign of a rescue party.

She dragged herself a couple of feet across the ground until she could dip her swollen wrist into the stream again. The water was so cold that it made her start shivering even more than she had been. But it was worth it, because it also numbed her arm instantly. Plus, it helped to wake her up and cleared her mind a little.

Tiny was still lying down. She watched Lisa carefully, nickering every few minutes with apparent concern.

"Don't worry, girl," Lisa said. "I'll be right back."

She kept her arm in the stream as long as she could stand it, staring at the water rushing by and wishing that

it was her familar Willow Creek instead of some unknown stream in some unknown forest. If she were on
the banks of Willow Creek right now, in The Saddle
Club's favorite rest spot on their favorite trail, that
would mean that Carole and Stevie would be coming
along to rescue her at any minute. Then she wouldn't
have a thing to worry about.

With a sigh, Lisa finally pulled her arm out of the
water and dried it carefully on her sweater. This wasn't
Willow Creek, and Stevie and Carole had no idea where
she was. Nobody did. Would anyone ever find her?

"WHERE DO YOU think Lisa is?" Stevie said for about the
tenth time.

Carole frowned. "I told you thirty seconds ago," she
said. "I don't know. Maybe she got held up at that girl's
house."

"Hmmm." Stevie stirred the melted remains of her
sundae with her spoon. "Well, at least the happy couple
is gone."

She had said that about ten times, too, but Carole
could understand why. She was also relieved about the
departure of Tate and Veronica. The pair had finally
impressed each other so much that they had walked out
arm in arm to go to the movies, leaving their ice cream
half finished.

But now Carole and Stevie had been sitting in TD's
for well over an hour.

"Do you think she forgot?" Stevie asked, glancing again at the clock on the wall.

"You already asked that," Carole said. "And I already said it's not very likely. When have you ever known Lisa to forget an appointment? Or even to be more than a few minutes late? Especially to a Saddle Club meeting."

Stevie shrugged. "Practically never," she said. "Maybe her bus is running late."

"It would have to be running *really* late," Carole pointed out. "It's only a twenty-minute ride from here to Colesford."

Stevie dropped her spoon and waved a hand at the waitress. "Well, I guess we should just be patient a little longer," she said. "But I'm going to need more food."

BY THE TIME another half hour had passed, Stevie had polished off a second sundae, and she and Carole were both getting very worried.

"It's pitch dark outside," Carole said. "She would have finished riding at least a couple of hours ago, right?"

Stevie shrugged. "Maybe she ended up hitting it off with that girl. What was her name again?"

"Um . . ." Carole thought for a second. "Margaret, was it? No, Marguerite. That was it. Marguerite Mills."

"Right," Stevie said. "Anyway, maybe she liked Marguerite so much that she changed her mind about coming home early and decided to stay."

"Maybe," Carole said doubtfully. "But she knew we were planning to meet her here. And you know Lisa—she's so responsible. She would never just stand us up. She would at least call."

Suddenly Stevie sat bolt upright in the booth. "Maybe that's it!" she exclaimed. "Maybe she left us a message at Pine Hollow and we just didn't get it. We did leave a little early to come here."

Carole looked hopeful. "Do you think that could be it?" she said. Before Stevie could respond, she answered her own question with a definite nod. "That's got to be it!" she said. "There's no other explanation."

"Come on, let's call the stable and find out," Stevie said, jumping to her feet and digging in her pocket for a quarter.

Red O'Malley picked up the phone at Pine Hollow. He said he hadn't heard a word from Lisa all day. Neither had Max or Mrs. Reg. Red even put Stevie on hold for a moment to call up to Max's house and check with Deborah. Nobody had received a call from Lisa.

Next the girls tried their own houses. Their parents reported that there had been no messages from their friend. Then the girls dialed Lisa's home number. There was no answer.

Stevie hung up and stared at Carole. "I don't like this," she said. "Where could she be?"

"We'd better try to call that girl, Marguerite," Carole

128

said. She was really starting to worry. She tried to tell herself that it was probably nothing, that Lisa must have just forgotten about their meeting. But that was so unlike Lisa that Carole couldn't make herself believe it.

Stevie picked up the phone again. It didn't take long to get the Millses' home number from directory assistance.

"Thank goodness they're listed," Carole commented. "A lot of times those rich, snooty people aren't."

Stevie just nodded and pressed the phone closer to her ear as it rang in the Millses' house. Two rings, three, four . . .

"Thank you for calling. Jeffrey, Roberta, and Marguerite aren't available to take your call right now, but . . ."

Stevie slammed the phone down in frustration before the recorded message could finish. "They're not there," she said. "I got the answering machine."

"What are we going to do?" Carole asked. "Do you think something is wrong?" All kinds of terrible images crowded into her mind. Lisa in a car accident. Lisa in a riding accident. Lisa getting sick and being rushed to the hospital . . . It was scary to be so positive that something was wrong but not to know anything for certain.

"I'm sure she's fine," Stevie said. "Her mom probably dragged her off to tea at the White House or something."

But Carole could tell by the frown on Stevie's face

that she didn't believe that any more than she did. "I've got it!" she said suddenly. "Why don't we call that stable? The one where she was supposed to go riding."

Stevie snapped her fingers, and her face brightened slightly. "Brilliant!" she said. "That should tell us something. Now, what was the name of it again?"

"Fox Crest Farms," Carole said promptly. "I remember it, because I'd never heard of it before." She smiled a little. "Also because it sounded like the kind of name that someone snobby like one of Lisa's mother's friends would think was classy."

Stevie was already dialing the number for directory assistance again. Soon she was waiting for someone to pick up at the stable.

"Hello?" said a bored-sounding male voice after several rings.

"Hello!" Stevie said. "Um, is this Fox Crest Farms?"

"Yeah," the voice replied. "Who're you calling for?"

"My name is Stevie Lake, and I—" Stevie cut herself off. This was no time for niceties like proper introductions. She started again. "I'm looking for a girl named Lisa Atwood."

"Sorry, never heard of her," the voice said. "You must have the wrong stable."

"Wait!" Stevie cried before the person could hang up. "You don't understand. She doesn't usually ride there. She was there this afternoon as the guest of someone named Marguerite Mills."

130

"Oh, Marguerite!" For the first time the voice sounded a little livelier. "Sure, she's a friend of mine. Hold on, she's just down the hall. I'll get her."

Stevie let out a sigh of relief as she heard the phone clatter down on the other end. She quickly filled Carole in on what was happening, then waited.

Finally she heard someone pick up. "Hello?" chirped a perky voice. "This is Marguerite. Who's this?"

"Hi there," Stevie said. "I'm a friend of Lisa's. Lisa Atwood."

"Oh." Marguerite didn't sound very impressed. "Yeah? She's not here anymore."

Stevie's heart sank. She realized that she had been hoping with all her might that Lisa would still be with Marguerite. "Are you sure?"

"Of course I'm sure," Marguerite said impatiently. "My friends and I have been hanging out here for hours now, and I haven't seen her. Besides, she said something about catching a bus back to Willow Creek."

"Yes," Stevie said, "but she's not here." She wasn't sure what else to say. "Um, do you happen to know which bus she was taking? What time, I mean?" She could see that Carole was listening breathlessly to her side of the conversation, fingers crossed on both her hands.

"I have no idea," Marguerite replied. "I think it was probably around three o'clock or so when we split up out in the woods, so—"

131

"Split up?" Stevie interrupted. Her mouth was dry all of a sudden. "What do you mean, split up? You left her out on the trail alone?" All of Max's lectures over the years about riding safety flashed into her mind. *Never ride alone. Always tell someone where you're going. Never ride alone. . . .*

"It's no big deal." Marguerite sounded irritated. "It was still broad daylight, you know. And it was only raining a little."

Stevie gulped. "Wait a minute, Marguerite. I need you to do something. Go and see if Lisa's horse is back."

"Oh, really," Marguerite said irritably. "Of course her horse is back. Look, I'm sure Lisa's on her way home. Just give it some time."

"Go and check on her horse," Stevie said firmly.

"I have things to do," Marguerite protested. "And anyway, my friends and I were just getting ready to leave."

"Go and look for the horse Lisa was riding," Stevie said again. "Do it *now*."

Marguerite sighed loudly and was silent for a moment. "Wait," she said at last. "Let me go check with one of the grooms first. Maybe someone else saw her come in, and then you can get off my back, okay?"

"Fine," Stevie said. She heard Marguerite drop the phone and hurry off. "You'd just better come back," she muttered.

"What's going on?" Carole demanded anxiously.

132

When Stevie told her what Marguerite had said, her eyes widened. "Oh no," she breathed. She looked at her watch. "She could have been out there for hours. Hurt, or . . ." She didn't finish the sentence.

Marguerite returned. "I just talked to the head groom," she said, sounding breathless and, for the first time, a little bit worried. "He hasn't seen Lisa. Plus, he said that Tiny—that's the horse she was riding—seems to be missing."

Now Stevie was really scared. "Listen, Marguerite," she said firmly. "We're coming over there right now. Stay put until we get there."

"What?" Marguerite started to protest.

Stevie didn't let her finish. "Lisa could be in trouble," she barked. "And it's your fault. Now we need you to stick around and help us out. We'll be there in twenty minutes."

This time Marguerite didn't argue. "Okay," she said in a small voice. "Um, let me give you directions. . . ."

Stevie dug a pen out of her jacket pocket and scribbled a few notes on a napkin. Then she cut the connection and started dialing a new number.

"Who are you calling now?" Carole asked.

"Red," Stevie replied grimly. "We need a ride to Colesford."

133

11

LISA CLUNG TO Tiny's neck with all the strength she had left. It wasn't much. She was wet and cold, and the woods around her were dark and empty. There was no telling how long she'd been out here. It felt like a lifetime. By now the pain in her back and leg was so familiar that she hardly bothered to think about it anymore.

"I'm so glad you're here, Prancer," she murmured, burying her face in the horse's warm neck. "You're the only friend I have left."

The horse snorted, and Lisa looked up. Her mind felt hazy, with deep, thick darkness creeping in at the corners. But she realized her mistake.

"Um, sorry," she mumbled. "Tiny. Your name's Tiny.

I'm sorry." Tears started to drip down her face along with the raindrops that were still falling. Lisa shook her head violently. It sent a sharp spasm of fresh pain down her spine, but for once she didn't mind. The pain woke her up a little, jolted her brain back into shape, and sent the darkness scurrying further back into the recesses of her mind.

She had to stay alert, had to concentrate on listening for rescuers or passersby. Was it ten o'clock yet? Had her parents realized she was missing? Or were they still dancing the night away at some fancy party?

Lisa didn't know, but she had to keep herself focused. She had to make sure her brain kept working so that the darkness wouldn't take it over entirely.

"Okay, Tiny," she said. "Listen up. I'm going to tell you everything you need to know about stable management. Here goes. . . ." She took a deep breath, trying to collect her thoughts. Her logical, well-trained brain had never let her down before.

"Okay," she said again. "First of all, we can talk about all the different breeds of horses. I don't know what breed you are, Tiny. But here are some of the breeds I know about. Let's see. There's Thoroughbreds, and Arabians, and quarter horses. And American Saddlebreds, and Morgans, and Shetland ponies, and Tennessee walking horses. Um, and Trakehners, Westphalians. Appaloosas. Lipizzaners." Lisa searched her mind. "Then there are palominos— oh, wait. I'm not sure if that's a breed or a color. Um, there's Arabians. Did I say that one already?"

Lisa wiped the rain out of her eyes and decided it was time to change to a new topic.

"All right, how about this," she told Tiny. "Did you know there are lots of different materials that can be used as bedding in stalls? Well, there are. There's straw, of course. Actually, there are different kinds of straw, like wheat straw and oat straw and a few other kinds. Then there are wood shavings—those are a good thing to use if your horse likes to eat his bedding, because most of them don't like it. Some people use shredded newspaper, or hemp, or even sand. Um, then there's sawdust, and, let's see . . . peat moss. Oh, and I heard that some people use peanut shells. Isn't that funny?" She paused, wondering whether it was funny or not. It was too hard to decide, so she let it go.

"Okay, what were we talking about again?" she murmured. She wiggled her sore foot a little. It was starting to go numb from the cold. But when she moved it, the pain woke it up again. "I have an idea," she said. "I'll tell you what color all the ribbons are at a horse show. Let's see. . . ."

This time it took her quite a few minutes to think of what she wanted to say. The darkness was coming back, and it was claiming more and more of her mind. Besides that, she was starting to wonder if she had ever been quite this sleepy. Suddenly nothing seemed more important than closing her eyes, resting her head on the nice big soft thing in front of her—what was it again? Oh yes, a horse.

"No!" Lisa said out loud. The sudden noise startled Tiny, who had dozed off. The horse let out a loud, harrumphing snort that brought Lisa back to full consciousness.

She couldn't let herself sleep. She had to stay alert or she might never get out of this.

"Ribbons," she said firmly. "Um, okay. First place is blue. Second is red. Third place is yellow. Fourth is—um—white."

Lisa paused to smother a yawn. She was so tired. So tired.

"Fifth place," she went on slowly. "Fifth is green, I think—no, wait, it's pink. Definitely pink. Green is for sixth. Seventh, um, purple, and then . . ."

She had trouble retrieving the next number. Her head swam with the effort.

"Oh, Tiny," she murmured. "I think you'd better take over now. I'm too tired. . . . But it's a brown ribbon. I'm sure it's brown. . . ."

She couldn't keep her head up anymore. It dropped forward onto Tiny's shoulder. Lisa's eyes closed. Tiny woke up again and snorted quizzically, but there was no answer except the sound of the steadily falling rain.

* * *

LATER—HOW MUCH LATER? There was no telling. Lisa's mind started to come back to her. Where was she? She was cold, she knew that. And sleepy. Very sleepy. Why wasn't she still sleeping?

A noise came. A loud noise, very close. A horse, snorting and grunting loudly.

The earth shifted beneath her. It moved, and she started to slide.

She caught herself just in time. It wasn't the earth moving—it was the horse. She had been sleeping against the horse, and now the horse was moving and making a lot of noise. Why was she making so much noise? It made it hard to sleep.

The horse quieted down again, and that was when Lisa became aware of another kind of noise. It was coming from farther away. Could it be . . . voices?

It was! Human voices. Was she dreaming? Or did she hear one of the voices calling her name?

"Stevie?" Lisa whispered. Her voice came out in a hoarse croak. She tried to make it louder. "Hello?" she said. But she could hardly hear herself above the noise of the rain and the stream.

The voices came again. They were in the woods, not far, but not near, either. Not near enough. Lisa knew that they could move on and never notice her lying there.

She still wasn't sure if this was a dream or real life, but

she had to find out. She had to get the people's attention.

Her own voice was no good at all. She had to go to them. She had to stand up.

She tried. She pushed her feet under her and shoved off the horse's side. For a second, she thought it had worked. She was standing!

Then she tried to take a step, and the pain shot through her again, so strong that it almost overwhelmed her completely. She let out a croaking cry as her back spasmed and her legs collapsed under her, sending her crashing to the ground.

Tiny let out a neigh. With a great effort of will, Lisa looked up at her. The horse was staring at her, seemingly agitated. As Lisa watched in exhaustion, Tiny clambered awkwardly to her feet and came toward her, neighing loudly and anxiously.

Then Lisa heard answering shouts. The voices had heard Tiny! They had heard her! They were coming. . . .

Seconds later, half a dozen riders on horseback burst out of the darkness toward her.

"Lisa!" cried one of them. It was Stevie.

Another was already dismounting and running toward her. "Here she is!" the figure cried.

"C-Carole?" Lisa murmured. It seemed too good to be true. She looked up at the others. All the riders had dismounted by now. One of them—could it really be Max?—was talking into a portable phone. Lisa thought she also saw Red and Marguerite. . . .

Carole and Stevie were kneeling at her side. Carole was unrolling a blanket, which she tucked around Lisa carefully. It felt warm and dry and very, very good.

"Lisa, what happened?" Stevie asked. Her worried face swam in Lisa's vision. "Can you tell us what's wrong?"

"Um, my leg hurts," Lisa said. But suddenly that didn't seem so important anymore. She looked over toward Red, who was holding Tiny by the bridle, calming her down. "Tiny saved me," Lisa said. "She was . . . um . . ."

Max joined the others at her side. "Don't try to talk now, Lisa," he said soothingly. He unfurled an umbrella and held it above her head to keep the rain off. "The paramedics are coming. Everything is going to be all right now. Just rest."

Lisa opened her mouth again. She wanted to tell them about Tiny, about how brave and wonderful the horse had been. But somehow the words just wouldn't come. Maybe Max was right. Her friends were here now. They would take care of everything. It was time to rest.

12

"Isn't she adorable?" Carole whispered.

Stevie and Lisa nodded. It was a Tuesday afternoon about two weeks later, and the three girls were leaning on the half door of Calypso's stall, watching the mare and her new baby filly. The foal had been born several days earlier. And as it turned out, Calypso hadn't had any problems foaling. She had done it all by herself, in the middle of the night, with no one there.

"I still can't believe Max slept through the whole thing," Lisa said.

Stevie grinned. "Me neither," she said. "I guess having a baby of his own taught him how to sleep through just about anything."

A week before the foal was born, Red and Max had

set up a cot in the next stall and started taking turns sleeping there in order to keep a close eye on Calypso. But Max had ended up sleeping soundly through the whole thing, waking up after it was all over and the foal was already nursing.

Carole smiled down at the tiny, long-legged foal sleeping in the straw at Calypso's feet. "I guess that just goes to show that you really can't predict these things," she said. "We thought Calypso was going to have trouble, but she had it all well in hand. Or is it well in hoof?"

Lisa laughed and leaned farther across the half door to give Calypso a pat on the rump. She felt light and free without the back brace she had been wearing since the night of her fall.

Her friends noticed, too. "You look good, Lisa," Carole said. "Does your back hurt?"

"Not really," Lisa said. She swung her arms and twisted gently from side to side at the waist to prove it. "I'm glad my doctor finally said I could stop wearing that brace yesterday. It helped my back a lot, but as the weather got warmer it was starting to make me itch. And the best part is, she said I could probably start riding again in a week or two if I take it easy at first."

"Does that mean your ankle's better, too?" Stevie asked. "And your wrist?"

Lisa shrugged. "Almost as good as new," she said, flexing both joints for her friends. "My doctor said they really weren't that badly hurt—not even sprained, just twisted and strained."

"Wait a minute," Carole said. "I thought that was what was wrong with your back."

Lisa laughed. "No, that was twisted and *wrenched*," she corrected.

"Whatever," Stevie said. "I'm just glad we found you before you were twisted and strained and wrenched and frozen."

Her tone was light, but both Carole and Lisa nodded seriously.

"Believe me, so am I," Lisa said. "I could hardly believe it when I heard your voices coming toward me. I thought I was dreaming—or maybe hallucinating." She smiled. "Oh, and while we're at it—I'm just glad Tiny is so talkative. If she hadn't called you over, who knows when you might have found me?"

Before the others could say anything, they heard loud voices coming down the aisle toward them. "Oh no," Stevie whispered with a groan. "It's the battle of the bores. And they're headed this way."

"Quick," Carole whispered. "We've got to hide!"

Without another word, the three girls silently opened the door of the stall and slipped inside. Calypso gave them a quizzical look, then turned and pointed her ears toward the aisle, where Tate's and Veronica's loud voices were getting even closer. The foal didn't wake up.

The Saddle Club crouched down behind the half door, pressing themselves against it just in case Tate or Veronica stopped to look inside the stall at the new foal.

"Anyway, as I was saying," Tate said loudly outside, "it's important to know all the different kinds of jumps you might encounter in a hunter class so that you're well prepared. For instance, there's the simple post-and-rail, the in-and-out, the stone wall, the Aachen oxer, the chicken coop, the white gate—"

"Speaking of white gates," Veronica interrupted, "did I mention that my parents and I had dinner last week at White Gates, that mansion over in Mendenhall? It was fabulous. They served caviar before dinner, and then . . ."

Her voice faded out of earshot, and the three girls stood up, grinning.

"Whew," Carole said. "It's a good thing they didn't stop to look at the foal. I don't think I could have kept myself from laughing out loud for another ten seconds."

"Same here," Stevie agreed wholeheartedly. "I almost lost it when I thought about Tate trying to jump a real hunter course. The way he rides, if he tried it he'd probably fall off at the first jump, whether it was a simple post-and-rail or anything else."

"Please," Lisa said, wincing a little. "Don't mention falling off, okay? It's a sensitive subject for me right now." But then she smiled so that her friends could see she was joking—mostly.

"Agreed," Stevie said. As the girls let themselves out of the stall, she glanced down the aisle in the direction Veronica and Tate had gone. "So who's winning the bragging contest between those two, anyway? I can't tell."

"I think they both think they're winning," Carole said with a chuckle. "But if you ask me, we're the real winners here. Those two have kept each other so busy lately that neither one of them has had any time left over to bother us!"

Stevie grinned. "So does that mean you're really and truly over your crush on Tate?"

Carole gave her a sour look. "Like I told you yesterday, and the day before, and the day before that," she said, "I never had a crush on Tate. Not really. I just thought he was smart and interesting. And nice-looking, of course."

"That sounds like a crush to me." Stevie waggled her eyebrows.

Carole sighed. "Well, now those two have a crush on each other. Tate even gave Veronica that hunting horn of his as a present." She rolled her eyes. "Since her family is so socially prominent and all, he thought she could use it."

"I know who really could have used it," Stevie said.

"Lisa. When she was lost in the woods, she could have blown it and—"

Lisa wasn't paying attention. "Look!" she interrupted. "She's waking up."

Carole and Stevie dropped their conversation and turned to see. The foal lifted her head off the straw, blinked, and looked around. Then she gave a big yawn.

"Hi there, Tiny!" Carole crooned.

Lisa smiled. She still liked hearing that name. After the foal was born, Max had asked for suggestions about what to name her. Lisa had spoken up immediately. She knew of one very special horse who deserved to have her name passed on to a new generation.

That reminded her. She didn't want to be late. "I'd better go," she said, glancing at her watch. "Now that my brace is off, I think I should be able to handle the public bus system. I'm going to take a ride over to Fox Crest and visit Tiny. I've only seen her once since the accident. But from now on, I'm going to make a habit of stopping by whenever I can." She patted her pocket, which was bulging with carrot sticks and other treats for the big gray horse.

"Want some company?" Carole asked.

Lisa smiled. "Sure," she said. "Are you sure you want to come?"

"Definitely," Stevie declared. "As long as you promise we don't have to stop and chat with Marguerite."

Lisa rolled her eyes. "Believe me, we won't," she said.

"I won't be upset if I never have to spend time with Marguerite Mills again, and I suspect that feeling is mutual. We're just not compatible." She called good-bye to Calypso and the new Tiny, then turned and headed down the aisle toward the locker room with her friends beside her. "Even my mother saw the light on that one."

"It sounds like your mother learned a lot from this whole thing, actually," Carole said. "She learned to appreciate how wonderful horses are—at least a little more, right?"

"Definitely," Lisa said. "At first she thought Tiny was to blame for my accident. But then I explained it to her, and she finally understood that Tiny probably saved my life. If I hadn't had her to keep me warm and to talk to . . ." She shuddered. "Let's just say that Mom thinks Tiny is a pretty special horse, too."

Stevie nodded. "And she thinks Pine Hollow is a pretty wonderful place, right?"

"Right," Lisa said. "I don't think she'll be dragging me off to ride at any more strange stables." For the first few days after Lisa's fall, Mrs. Atwood had tried to convince Lisa to give up riding entirely. Lisa hadn't paid her any attention. Instead, she had patiently explained over and over again that all riders fall off sometimes, and that accidents could happen to anyone. She had also been careful to tell her mother why she wouldn't have ended up in such dire circumstances if she had been riding at Pine Hollow. The riders there knew better than to ride

147

alone out on the trail, and besides that, she would have had The Saddle Club looking out for her.

Lisa smiled at that thought. The Saddle Club *had* looked out for her. They'd just had to go a little farther than usual to do it. And they'd had someone else helping them.

"What?" Stevie demanded, noticing Lisa's expression as the girls entered the locker room. "What's so funny?"

"Oh, nothing," Lisa replied. "I was just thinking about how Tiny took care of me out there. Now it's my turn to take care of her, by visiting her and showing her how much I appreciate what she did."

Stevie nodded and grabbed her backpack out of her cubby. "That's why Carole and I should come along with you on this visit. It sounds a lot like a Saddle Club project."

Lisa's eyes widened. "You know, it does," she said slowly. "In fact, now that I think about it, it almost feels like Tiny is a member of The Saddle Club. I mean, she fits the rules, right? You could say she's horse-crazy, I guess. But more importantly, she helped me out when I needed it."

Carole and Stevie exchanged glances. Then they both started to smile. "You know, you're right," Carole said, quickly pulling on her sneakers and stuffing her boots into her cubby. "When you put it that way, maybe The Saddle Club has a lot more members than just the three of us, and Phil and Emily and Kate and all the other out-of-town members. Human members, I mean."

By now, Stevie had broken into a full-fledged grin. "Absolutely," she said. "The Saddle Club has lots more members—really important members. In fact, the club couldn't exist without them! Members like Tiny and Belle and Starlight and Prancer—"

"And Barq and Samson and Topside and Patch and Diablo," Carole added. "And Calypso and her baby."

Lisa linked her arms through those of her two best friends as they all left the locker room. "And don't forget Chocolate and Berry and Stewball and Geronimo and Moonglow and Teddy and Jasper and Monkeyshines and Maverick and Eve . . ."

As she paused for breath, her friends added more names. Lisa knew that their extended membership list was just getting started. And she thought that that was absolutely, positively, *horstupendously* wonderful!

ABOUT THE AUTHOR

Bonnie Bryant is the author of nearly a hundred books about horses, including The Saddle Club series, Saddle Club Super Editions, and the Pony Tails series. She has also written novels and movie novelizations under her married name, B. B. Hiller.

Ms. Bryant began writing The Saddle Club in 1986. Although she had done some riding before that, she intensified her studies then and found herself learning right along with her characters Stevie, Carole, and Lisa. She claims that they are all much better riders than she is.

Ms. Bryant was born and raised in New York City. She still lives there, in Greenwich Village, with her two sons.

Don't miss Bonnie Bryant's next exciting
Saddle Club adventure . . .

ROCKING HORSE
The Saddle Club #77

It's time for the Willow Creek Junior High spring
dance. Since it's open to everyone, The Saddle Club
will be there, and so will Stevie's boyfriend, Phil Marsten. Unfortunately, Veronica diAngelo will be going
to the dance, too. The Saddle Club girls are determined not to let Veronica ruin their fun. But Veronica has her own plans. She arranges for The Saddle
Club to be stuck at Pine Hollow Stables the night of
the dance—taking care of her horse, Danny.

But Veronica is the one who's in for a surprise. Not
only do Carole, Stevie, and Lisa go to the dance, but
they take Danny with them, proving once and for all
that he's a horse with a rock-and-roll soul.

Saddle Up For Fun!
Join The Saddle Club

As an official Saddle Club member you'll get:

- *Saddle Club newsletter*
- *Saddle Club membership card*
- *Saddle Club bookmark*
- *and exciting updates on everything that's happening with your favorite series.*

Bantam Doubleday Dell Books for Young Readers
Saddle Club Membership Box BK
1540 Broadway
New York, NY 10036

SKYLARK

Bantam Doubleday Dell
Books for Young Readers

Name _____

Address _____

City _____ State _____ Zip _____

Date of birth _____